CW01424447

Below

"A chilling, thrilling and claustrophobic descent into the bowels of the earth. Past and present collide as Nick Jones, faces his fears, and goes in search of the story of his grandfather—the man after whom he was named. With terrific pacing and engaging characters, this dark story also shows how a spark of humanity can remain—even in the most monstrous form. Harrison's well-judged pacing and atmospheric skill bury you in the story as if you were one of the explorers yourself. But at least you can escape—can't you?"

– Stephanie Ellis, author of
The Five Turns of the Wheel and *As The Wheel Turns*

"Tight and claustrophobic, *Below* is another winner from Harrison"

– David Watkins, author of
Rhitta Gawr and *The Original's Return*

Below

by
Kev Harrison

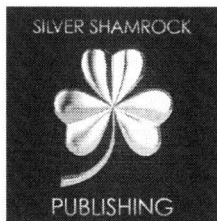

SILVER SHAMROCK

PUBLISHING

CW	CONTENT WARNINGS
	This book may contain content that triggers undesired reactions.
	CANNIBALISM, KIDNAPPING

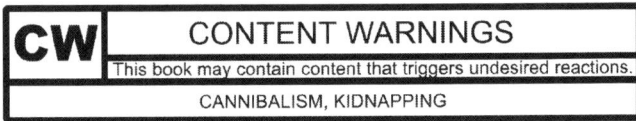

Copyright © 2021 Kev Harrison

Front Cover Design by Kealan Patrick Burke
Interior art by Bob Veon
Formatted by Kenneth W. Cain
Edited by Kenneth W. Cain

All rights reserved.

This is a work of fiction. Names, characters, businesses, places, events and incidents are either the products of the authors' imagination or used in a fictitious manner. Any resemblance to actual persons, living or dead, or actual events is purely coincidental.

No part of this publication may be reproduced, stored in a retrieval system, or transmitted in any form or by any means, without the prior permission in writing of the publisher, nor be otherwise circulated in any form of binding or cover than that in which it is published and without a similar condition including this condition being imposed on the subsequent purchaser.

"What you call darkness is not what a cat calls darkness, not what an owl calls darkness. Your reality is yours alone and only cousin to the reality of other creatures. Think of all the self-contained worlds and alien landscapes that prowl and glide just beyond your dark windows."

— Jarod K. Andersen

CHAPTER ONE

Nick shuffled in his seat, thrilled at this chance to make a lifelong dream come true, and simultaneously dreading the days ahead, below ground, in the dark. He loosened his seatbelt and glanced out of the window for the third time, beyond the boarding sleeve and into the terminal. A barrier of fluffy clouds loomed overhead as daylight ebbed away. He checked his watch. Three minutes until departure.

Where is she?

A flight attendant stopped in the aisle. "Excuse me, sir. Would you mind tightening your seatbelt for me? We'll be taking off shortly."

He smiled, pulling the belt tighter. He felt beads of sweat form on the back of his neck and twisted the cool air nozzle above his head. He closed his eyes, the breeze calming him.

"Nick?"

The posh-sounding accent brought him straight back to the now. He opened his eyes, dazzled by the brightness of the woman's smile, tanned skin and dark lipstick highlighting the whiteness of her immaculate teeth.

"Jess?" He offered his hand.

She leaned in, air kissing him on both cheeks, the fragrance of coconut heavy in her braided hair. She planted herself into her seat and took out her phone, thumbing through menus.

"I thought you were going to miss the fli—"

"Hold on," she said, index finger over her lips, schoolteacher-esque. She angled the phone. "Hi, guys. Here I am aboard this beautiful 787 Dreamliner on my way to San Francisco for Adventure Travel TV. I am *so* excited. Let me introduce you to my co-presenter, Nick. Say hi, Nick."

Nick froze, confused, then waved into the camera.

She continued, "I have to switch to flight mode now, but I'll be bringing you all the news and behind-the-scenes action from our show once we arrive. Have a great day. Love you guys." She pouted, making a kissing sound, and then pressed the round, red 'stop' button on the screen. She thumbed expertly through a sequence of screens until the video had been shared on her page.

"Sorry about that," she said, stuffing the phone into the pouch on the back of the seat in front and kicking off her sandals.

"What *was* that?" Nick tried his best not to look too horrified.

"Got to keep my viewers informed the whole time. Seriously, if I don't do an update for, like, twenty-four hours, I'll be five k down. It's such a pain in the arse, but it pays for...well, everything, so...you know?" Jess shrugged her shoulders.

Nick nodded. "Fair enough."

The plane juddered backwards from the terminal. Jess clipped her seatbelt into place and sat back. Nick pulled out a folder from the seatback and opened it, pulling out a crinkled newspaper clipping, his fingertips absentmindedly circling next to the bearded man in the centre of the sepia photo.

Jess leaned in. "Is that him?"

"The last photo taken of him before…"

Jess squeezed his arm. "Must be weird. Your grandfather being a hero you never met."

"It is. But that's why we're going. My chance to see where he lived, what he did, where he…where it ended."

Jess released her grip on his arm. "He was a bit of a role model for you, eh?"

"He's the reason I ended up doing what I do. My grandma was always so full of stories from back in Wales and down in Cornwall when I was growing up. He died at twenty-eight, but he'd already lived this incredibly adventurous life, underground." Nick slipped the photo back into the folder, pulling out a modern map in its place. He folded the page back, revealing a copy of an old sketch diagram. A mine plan.

Jess leaned into him. "I've got one of those, too. The map, not the drawing." She tugged her rucksack from under the seat in front and pulled out her own map. "I've never been to San Fran before. After we finish shooting, I'm going to go and play tourist, get some cute pics with some seals, up the coast. That'll bag another few hundred followers, for sure. How long is the drive to…Mariposa?"

Nick studied the map. Did some mental maths. "It looks like a couple hundred miles on the map, so probably three hours. Maybe more if the trucks are fully loaded with gear. I hope I can get some sleep on this flight."

The plane rolled to a stop. Nick pressed his cheek to the window. "Here we go," he said, easing the belt away from his waist. The noise of the jets firing filled the air. Nick sat back, his fingers digging into the armrests as though his life depended on it.

Jess, too, leaned back. "Not a good flyer?" she said, facing straight ahead.

"It's not flying, exactly. I'm just claustrophobic."

She sat forward as the plane's ascent levelled off and the roar of the engines reduced to a drone. "Claustrophobic? You *do* know we're going to explore a collapsed gold mine, right?"

Nick chuckled nervously. "It seems ridiculous, I know. I'll keep it together. I've already been to an old silver mine in Cornwall as preparation. But yeah…before this, I was a desk man. Mining engineering PhD. Most of it was theoretical—very little time actually spent underground. But I'll be fine." He turned to Jess. "Anyway, you know my story. How about you? What lured you into the project?"

The aircraft banked to the left, gaining height as London's monuments shrunk until they were obscured beneath the wall of cotton wool clouds. Nick pushed himself back into his seat, hands gripping the armrests tightly as he gazed out of the window. He felt Jess move closer, invading his personal space. Night was falling, the sky a washed-out deep blue.

The plane levelled off, and Jess stuffed her map back into her bag, before taking her mobile from the seat pocket and holding it up.

"There's only so long my career can be *this*. The intensity, the need to be always on, to never drop an f-bomb, to never look like shit—even at seven in the morning. Nah. No thanks. So, when Adventure Travel TV gave me the call about finding your grandpa, exploring the shafts—even the museum project after—I was in! This is my big break into TV, Nick. I *have to* make it work."

The seatbelt light dimmed with a gentle beep. Nick gratefully unclipped his belt and sighed.

Jess followed suit. "Better?" she said.

He murmured affirmatively, wiping a film of sweat from his forehead.

Jess turned to the aisle, raising her hand to a passing flight attendant. "Excuse me, are you going to be serving drinks soon?"

The man took a step back, adjusted his tie. "Yes, madam. The bar will come around for pre-dinner drinks in a few minutes. What would you like?"

She held up two fingers. "Two glasses of champagne please." She turned back to Nick and winked.

Nick forced a smile and nodded to the attendant to confirm the order.

Dinner was a quieter affair, their seatback entertainment screens blaring colourful images at them. Jess watched a documentary about a woman kayaking the length of the Amazon River while Nick chose a sitcom, trying to relax. They chased their meals with brandy and scotch, respectively, then Nick reclined his seat, inserted his ear buds, and reduced the sound of the cabin to a wonderfully indistinct hum.

Jess' fingers gently tapped his shoulder. "Sleep tight," she mouthed to him.

"You too," he said, and closed his eyes.

CHAPTER TWO

Dawn hadn't quite broken when they touched down in San Francisco. Mechanically collecting their baggage, few words passed between them. They emerged into the arrivals hall and soon found the driver with their names on a placard who led them to a minibus. The bustling traffic of the city—even before 5:00 a.m.—soon gave way to quieter towns, villages, and eventually wide expanses of nothing. Nick was struck by the dryness of everything, the soil parched. The trees that lined the city's boulevards were soon replaced by cacti, standing to attention amid the dusty landscape.

He felt a tap on his shoulder and turned to find Jess awake and pointing her phone camera between the front seats, towards a mountain range up ahead, lush with tall trees. The first fragments of daylight cracked the sky at uneven angles between the peaks. Nick smiled, in spite of Jess' inane commentary. Even feeling as shattered as he did, it was quite a sight.

"Almost there," called the driver from in front. "We'll pass through Mariposa and a little ways up into the mountains, near Midpines. That's where the mine is. Well, *was*." He laughed out loud.

Nick wondered where he got his energy at this time of day.

After fifteen minutes of rattling around tightly curved mountain tracks, they pulled off the road and into a makeshift parking lot. It was close to 7:00 a.m. and the sun was shining brightly from behind a thin haze of cloud overhead. There were four long trailers, gleaming in the morning light at angles from one another and a short, balding man in a suit and sunglasses, waiting for them.

They stepped down from the van and approached him, Nick extending his hand in greeting.

"Good morning. Great to meet you in person at last," the man said. "I'm James."

Nick shook his hand firmly "Good to meet you too." He stepped aside as Jess approached, leaning in for more air kisses. "So, what's the plan? Studio work first for intros and back story?" Nick glanced one way and the other. "Are we doing them in the trailers?"

James took off his shades and began to polish them with a handkerchief. "Well, we talked about it and, as we have our own studios down in Los Angeles, we can do that whenever. We're going to go straight into the mine. Our diggers will arrive in a couple of hours with the film crew. I wanted to be here to let you know, personally, about the change of plans. Right now, though, I guess you'll both be grateful for the chance to put your head down, then grab a shower. So, let me give you these." He stepped forward, handing Jess and Nick keys.

"They're fully equipped, all mod cons. We've stocked your fridges and cupboards with enough food for the full two weeks, if we end up staying that long. There's a watercooler in Sofia's trailer—she's the camera operator—but unless I'm forgetting something, I think you're all set."

Nick rubbed his mop of dark, wavy hair, then looked over at Jess.

She grinned. "A nap and a shower sounds perfect." She walked over to the trailer with her name on the door and took a snap on her phone camera, then fiddled with the lock until the door swung open. She whistled as she looked in, then spun around. "Will you be staying here with us, James?"

"Me? Nah. But as head of production on the series, we'll have a conference call every night when shooting stops." He stepped over towards Nick, put his hand on his shoulder. "I'm really looking forward to seeing what we can do with this, Nick. Not to mention the legacy project of the museum. It's a wonderful idea, and with your expertise and Jess' energy..." He stepped back, checking his watch. "Listen, I've got a conference call in about twenty minutes about another show, so I'm going to jump back in my car and scoot. But if you need something, call, okay? Diego will make sure you both have my number."

The minibus driver gave a thumbs-up as he took a drag of his cigarette.

Nick grasped the strap of his rucksack and hauled it over to the trailer. "See you in a couple hours," he said, and disappeared inside.

Nick came to with the sound of heavy tyres crunching the rocky surface outside. He lifted himself from the face-down position he'd conked out in and felt the stickiness of the sweat that bound his t-shirt to his chest. He cursed himself as he noticed the aircon unit overhead, still switched to off. He quickly undressed, then stepped into the narrow shower cubicle. Water blasted his body, icy cold, at first shocking but then delightfully refreshing.

He stepped out of the shower, towelled himself off, and slung on a clean t-shirt with the same lightweight trousers. The daylight dazzled him despite his sunglasses as he stepped outside. A sharp cry overhead drew his gaze; a huge bird of prey soared in an otherwise empty sky. Jess was standing next to the bulky truck which had just arrived, talking animatedly in Spanish to Diego and a petite woman with cropped hair and a shoulder cam that Nick guessed was Sofia.

Nick strolled over. "*Buenas dias*," he said.

Jess angled her head. "You speak Spanish?"

Nick chuckled. "That was about fifty percent of my repertoire, sorry."

Sofia grinned and covered the two paces between them, enthusiastically reaching out a hand. "Nice to meet you," she said.

"Pleasure is mine," Nick said, still feeling the lack of sleep. "So, if everyone's here, when do we get started?"

Sofia nodded over Nick's shoulder. "They're already at it. Following your plans to the letter, so James said."

Nick turned and saw a large drill and an earthmover sitting beside a collapsed wooden structure. Nick turned back to the others. They read the urgency on his face, and the three of them scrambled up the shallow incline towards the machines.

"Stay back there, please," came a voice. A man wearing a hard hat and hi-vis jacket emerged from behind the earthmover. "It should be safe from what we know about the cave-in, but we don't want to take any risks."

Nick dashed forward, waving. "I'm Nick Jones. The engineer who planned the operation. From the university in North Wales?"

The man sped up his pace, almost jogging towards Nick. "Dr. Jones, great to meet you."

"Nick, please. And you are?"

"Alvin Matthews, chief engineer on the project. But call me Al. I've got a spare hard hat and goggles up here near the drill. Come with me."

Nick turned to the others, gesturing for them to stay put, then moved in step with Al as he approached the collapsed entrance. Al reached up onto the cluttered dash of the drilling machine and pulled down Nick's blueprint. He began describing the physical features in front of them to the key points on the rock face. Nick listened and watched, nodding along as he related the 3D image on the paper to the reality in front.

"Shall we do this?" Al's excitement had ratcheted up as he explained the process.

Nick rubbed his hands together, excited. "Let's."

Al waved to the man at the controls of the drill. He drove the drill forward, boring into the rock face, the wind whipping dust and debris away to the east.

Sofia and Jess retreated into the shade of Sofia's trailer, waiting and talking.

After somewhere close to two hours, Nick hurried down the side of the hill and called out, "Guys, let's get the camera ready. We're in. After sixty-one years, we're inside the mine. Come on!"

Sofia stepped down from the trailer first, attaching clip-on mics to Nick's t-shirt and Jess' vest top. They each stuffed battery packs into their pockets and tested them before setting off back up the hill to the entrance.

The drill machine had been pulled back a few yards to give them space, while the earthmover stood with its scoop aloft, filled with rocky debris. Chunks of aged, splintered wood jutted out at odd angles.

Sofia hoisted her shoulder-cam into filming position and turned to Al. "You sure it's safe?"

He peered into the gloom, the golden sunlight somehow swallowed by the blackness, no more than a yard inside. He turned back. "I'd prefer it if you would go no more than a few yards for now. Just until we can get some hydraulic supports in."

Sofia nodded, then turned to Nick. "This is your baby, Nick. Shall we?"

Nick stepped forward, reaching out with one hand and touching the arched entryway. "Are we rolling, Sofia?" he said.

"We are."

Nick took in a deep breath and stepped over the threshold. "This is the first time that anyone has been inside this mine since the collapse on May 12th, 1957. Our team has just drilled our way in, so we're only able to show you the entryway for now, but we are standing in perfectly preserved histo-" He felt something slip under his foot and reached for the wall for balance.

Nick crouched. The light of Sofia's camera followed, first illuminating his face, then his folded body and onward to his feet. Sofia gasped. Beside Nick's left boot was a hand. Rather, the bones which once made up a hand. A splintered fragment of a radius bone lay inches away and, as Nick got closer, he could see that the thumb and the two bones that would have supported it had been crushed.

"This is from the original cave-in." He was talking to himself. "This could be... I need to go back outside."

Nick stood, his skin a shade whiter. Sofia followed him with the camera, asking him more than once if he was okay. Jess grabbed his arm at the elbow and led him out into the daylight. They stood quietly for a moment, Nick's breathing short, his eyes struggling to focus.

Jess reached out, touching Sofia's shoulder. "Do you want me to do the intro? If he's...you know?"

Sofia shook her head. "I think we should just give him time. The diggers need to secure the entry tunnels anyway. Let's try again in a few hours." She glanced at Nick. "I hope he's going to be up to this."

CHAPTER THREE

The stink of earth hung heavy in the air. The light was dim, but a world away from the impenetrable black of earlier in the day. Of when Nick had found the bones. Hydraulic jacks held up the corridor, though it seemed stable enough without them. Nevertheless, the security they imparted on the group was welcome.

"Can you imagine what it must've been like, working in here? I'm five foot ten and I have to crouch to walk." Jess paced behind Sofia, who followed Nick further into the mine shaft. "And is it always this hot?"

"It's actually going to get *much* hotter," Nick called back. "The deeper beneath the surface we get, the higher the pressure. The temperature will rise accordingly."

"Thank God I'm wearing shorts," Jess said.

Sofia sniggered.

The drilling machine had made heavy work of the first seventy yards, then discovered an intact section of the mine, leading to three descending tunnels. Al's men had been inside, placing hydraulic supports and fluorescent tube lights while Nick took time out. After six or seven minutes inside, the crunching texture of newly drilled rock gave way to smoother, older terrain. Footsteps quietened until the sound was unnoticeable, nothing more than the rhythmic heartbeat of their march.

"Stop," said Jess, her breath short.

Nick turned to face her. "Are you okay? Getting tired?"

She held up her right hand, shook her head. "Not that. Listen, you hear that?"

Sofia held one cup of her headphones tight to her left ear. "I'm not getting any—wait." She paused, her facial expression scrunched in concentration. "It's like a...a clicking or something."

"Exactly!" Jess took a step towards Sofia. "Can you tell where it's coming from?"

"I can't be sure, but it sounds like it's from that wall. And up high." She angled the camera to her left, rotating a dial to engage night vision, and scanned the wall. Jagged lines of rock and soil were vivid on-screen, like a contour map of some nightmare kingdom. Everything was still.

Then movement.

A shimmering, bi-coloured carapace shifted one way and the other, as spindly legs bent and shifted, propelling the beetle across the wall, towards a deep crack. "Hey little fella," said Sofia, zooming in.

"What is it?" Jess leaned in to get a better look at the screen.

"Looks to me like a click beetle. Curious thing is, these things usually only live near fresh water. I wonder how long it's been down here."

"Guys," Nick called from just ahead. "I've found passages down to the lower levels."

Sofia switched the camera mode back to normal, and they hurried to where Nick was standing. Wooden signs, still nailed into the wall, stood as testament to the history of the place. The paint, in various shades of white, red, and gold, was faded, almost illegible. The first sign read "Trucks only." A rusted section of narrow-gauge rails trailed off into the darkness below. The second sign read "Diggers," with an arrow pointing ahead and downward. The light from the shaft behind them was dim, almost useless from where they stood.

Nick reached into his small rucksack and pulled out a head torch. He fitted it around his hard hat and twisted, cold halogen light spewing forth and casting the path ahead into bright visibility.

"Shall we head down? Take a look?" Nick's enthusiasm betrayed him, his voice energised with excitement.

"Let's shoot an update here before we do. Jess, come past me, stand with Nick. Let's do this with both of you."

Jess squeezed through the cramped tunnel, her eyes searching the wall for more insects before she allowed herself to get closer. Sofia took a step back and silently counted down from five on her fingers, her camera trained on them both. She gave a thumbs-up as she reached zero.

Jess grinned into the camera and began to speak. "So, we've made it to the end of the first tunnel here in the mine. Behind us, you can see the *original* signs, meant for the miners who tragically died here all those years ago in 1957."

Nick adjusted the brightness on his head torch and picked up where Jess left off. "Earlier today, after our dig team cut through the rock face for the first time in over *sixty* years, we actually found some human remains, and…and, at this stage, it's impossible for us to know if they might have been my heroic grandfather." Jess' gently rubbed his arm below the shoulder. He inhaled and stepped back. "This is the sign Jess was telling you about. You can see this one here points to the truck tunnel which—"

"Nick, stop. Wait a second." Jess held her arm up to shield herself from the torchlight. She stepped forward. "You see this? Sofia, can you see this? Get closer. Oh my God. Oh my God." She reached across to something moving, attached to the sign. A piece of paper. Material from the edges had been eaten away at by time and insects, but as Nick's eyes scanned it, they settled on the name at bottom of the paper.

"Nicholas Jones? It's not possible. Give it to me a moment."

His head torch shone down on to the paper, brightly illuminating it. The surface was stained brown but written in a looping hand, in faded blue ink, was a journal entry of sorts. He shook his head, felt a sudden dryness in his throat.

"Sofia, are we still recording?" The camera moved up and down in a nodding motion. "I'm just going to read this…read what I can make out, okay?" He took a breath, forced his eyes closed, then opened them again.

> *To anyone that may happen upon this journal, such as it is.*
>
> *Today is May 12th, 1957. We experienced an earthquake, said to be far worse than any previous cases since the mine's opening. The entryway collapsed as we were removing a wagon. I, with the help of Robert from back home, convinced two of our American colleagues to support the beams and boulders until the rest of the miners could make their way out.*
>
> *There wasn't time for us, and the entire tunnel came down. One American lad, Jeffrey, got his arm caught under the rubble. We tried to lift it but to no avail and, eventually, as the most experienced here, I decided to remove the arm with the end of a pick. There's a lot of blood. The boy is still unconscious, but we have moved*

him—and ourselves—to the relative safety of the mining floor below.

Nicholas Jones

"I think that's enough for today, don't you?" Jess looked at Sofia, who nodded.

"He was still alive," Nick said to no one in particular.

"We should preserve that letter. It's a museum piece, for sure." Jess held out her hand.

Nick stared at her, his lips trembling, slightly parted. He handed her the paper and followed her to the exit.

Sunset was painted in vivid streaks of red and purple, long shadows climbing the hill from the trailers to the mine entrance. It had been an intense day, for which the two bottles of wine in Jess' fridge had proved the ideal antidote. Nick's eyes were heavy as he drained what was left of his third glass.

"What time is it?" he said over the crackling of the fire they'd built in front of the three trailers.

Jess glanced at her chunky sports watch. "Ten to midnight, almost."

Nick placed his glass on the ground beside his camping chair. "No, no. I mean in London. What time is it *for us*?"

Sofia chuckled. "Shit, guys, it's almost 8:00 a.m. for you."

Nick scooped his glass from the ground and stood, strolling towards his trailer. He turned. "That's it for me, folks. I need some sleep. Tomorrow is going to be a huge day."

The two of them raised their glasses to him and wished him a good night.

Nick brushed his teeth and climbed into bed where the low murmur of the conversation outside provided the perfect backdrop to help him doze off.

CHAPTER FOUR

Nick's eyes flicked open, the frame of the trailer rattling. He could hear the low, persistent rumbling of the earth beneath him, accompanied by the high pitch of crockery shaking in cupboards in the kitchenette. Outside, it was still pitch dark, the only light inside the tiny blue pinprick of light from a notification on his phone. He reached out for it, swiping it to life. 3:37 a.m. He flicked away the notifications and turned on the torch, illuminating the confined space. He reached for his clothes and dressed quickly.

As he stepped down from the trailer, two moths darted towards him, dancing in the beam from his phone. Still the ground shook. He stared at the visible trembling of the huge trailer, before his eyes darted up the hillside to the mine.

What if the entrance has collapsed again?

He scrambled up the hillside, the beam from his flashlight app flicking one way, then the other. As he reached the top, he shone it over to the entrance and felt relief as the portal stood open, a great mouth of all-consuming darkness. The earthquake ended and the world was momentarily silent.

Rocks shifted under moving soil, below. He spun, torchlight scanning the hillside until it found the slender shape of Jess, following in his footsteps.

"Is the entrance okay?" she called out, one hand held up, protecting her from the light.

"It's fine. The hydraulics held," Nick shouted back.

Jess lowered her body to the ground, using her hands for balance as she made her way up the last few yards, then reached out a hand.

Nick pulled her to the top, where she stood, regaining her breath. "Didn't you bring a light?"

Jess shrugged. "I felt the ground rumbling and panicked. I just bolted up here. My night vision isn't too bad, anyway." She walked past Nick and on towards the mine entrance. "Bring the light over, would you?" she said, beckoning.

Nick followed, trying not to dazzle her. He shone the beam over the surface of the rock surrounding the entrance. Everything was still. No additional rubble adorned the entryway. The dull steel of the first hydraulic supports reflected the torchlight dimly back at them.

"That's a relief," Jess said, stepping backwards. "When I woke up, I thought—"

A clanging sound peeled from the entrance. Metal against metal. Distant, ever fainter echoes following the sound to their ears. Their eyes met.

"What the *fuck*?" Jess' expression twisted into one of fear. "Did that come from inside?"

Nick took a step into the mine. "It sounded like it." He swept the cone of light in an arc from left to right. Nothing moved. "It could have been debris, deeper in the—"

Clang. Clang. More sounds. Similar to the first, but this time the two were distinct, their echoes trailing behind.

"Like Knockers," Nick said under his breath. He felt the presence of Jess, close behind him.

"What did you say?" she whispered.

"Knockers," he said again.

Jess grasped his wrist firmly, directing the torchlight onto her face and casting shadows which highlighted her look of fear and annoyance. "Care to enlighten me?"

He tugged back the torchlight. "In Wales and some parts of the West Country, miners believe there are mythical creatures—Knockers—who cause mischief in the mines. They're detectable by…well, by knocking, like what we just heard." Jess' hard expression remained. "It's stupid folklore, Jess. From a scientific perspective, it's much more likely to be temperature or pressure differences causing metal, rock, or whatever to expand and contract. Relax."

Clang. Clang-clang-clang. A single noise, followed by three more in quick succession.

Jess stared into Nick's eyes. "Metal, expanding?" She raised an eyebrow as if waiting for him to react.

Another sound. High pitched, throaty. Impossible to discern whether animal or human.

He swallowed, his throat dry, then glanced back over his shoulder. "Let's just go back to the trailers, call it a night, yeah?"

Nick angled the torch out over the steep hillside, then led the way down to the base.

CHAPTER FIVE

Nick woke violently, cracks of bright light streaming in behind the blackout blinds in the lounge of his trailer. The clear air carried a different fragrance as it wafted in through the vents in the roof. Something edible. His stomach growled. He tugged on the clothes from the day before and stepped outside.

Sofia's trailer door was wide open. He could see her and Jess, sat at the small table inside, eating.

"Hey, sleepy!" Sofia called out. "Come and have some huevos rancheros!"

Nick's stomach roared again, and he jogged over to her trailer, squeezing in beside Jess, who was busily filming the feast for her followers. Sofia stood and laid eggs on top of the warm tortilla, garnishing the plate with chunky tomatoes and avocado.

"This looks amazing," he said, picking up his cutlery and digging in.

"Mmmm…it…mmm…it is," mumbled Jess, her mouth half full.

Sofia planted a jug of coffee and a bottle of high fat creamer in front of Nick.

He nodded, grateful, and continued to pile food into his mouth. He chewed, placing his cutlery back down, then swallowed. "Today's a big day. Al's team were laying guide ropes to help us out on the descent, before they left last night. It's just us now. But it's exciting to get down into the heart of things." He went back to slicing his food.

"I can't wait to get down there," Sofia said, stacking her empty plate onto Jess'. "But I wanted to hear a little about last night. The earthquake?" Her eyes flicked from Jess to Nick and back again.

Jess cupped her hands around her coffee mug and stared into the liquid. "We went up there to check that the entrance was okay. Well, Nick went first, I followed. Then when we were up there, we…we heard something."

Nick choked on a piece of tortilla and coughed loudly, waving his right hand as he took a large gulp of coffee. "We heard the sounds that features—natural and manmade—make when temperatures differ as wildly as they do out here. That's all."

Jess shot him a hard look. "After the knocking though. There was something—"

"Metal fatigue. Wood stretching. Who knows?" Nick beamed a deliberate smile at Sofia.

Silence descended over the table.

Sofia stood and added Nick's plate to the pile, carrying them to the small sink in the kitchenette.

"No no no," said Nick. "If you handle breakfast duty, I'm washing up."

Sofia stood back, hands raised in defence. "No problem for me," she said, moving back to the table. "What time shall we head underground?" she asked as she perched on the edge.

Nick splashed soapy water around with a scrubbing brush on the plates. "Let's say…half an hour's time. What do you think?" He glanced over at Jess.

She nodded but said nothing.

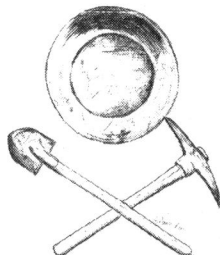

Nick was wearing a fresh change of clothes and hiking boots. He led them in, testing their head torches and the satellite phone. Sofia double-checked her two additional battery packs for her camera, then they entered the cool darkness of the mine shaft.

The corridor that made up the entrance had been all but cleared of debris which, in combination with the overhead lighting, made the tunnel almost hospitable. They arrived at the downward tunnels within minutes.

As promised, guide ropes lined the rightmost tunnel, fed through eye bolts secured to the walls. The path down was steep and less cleanly cut, with edges of rock jutting out at odd intervals. Al's team had done their best to place lighting units where they could, but the uneven rock face had made it difficult.

Nick felt his underarms flush with heat, sweat beading on his neck and forehead as the space narrowed and light dimmed. "I'm going to turn on my head torch, guys," he said over his shoulder. "It's best if only one of us lights up at once. Conserve battery." He twisted the lens of the torch and a cone of light spread out in front of him, illuminating a fine rain of dust.

Jess and Sofia murmured their acknowledgement and edged closer to him to benefit from the improved illumination.

After almost ten minutes of difficult descent, they found themselves in the first digging chamber of the mine. Away to their right, they could just make out the lower end of the narrow-gauge railway, a single car waiting for cargo that would never come, the fabric of its wooden sides darkened and torn with decay.

Sofia fired up the camera. "Let's do a bit here," she said as light began to stream from the lamp above the lens. She directed the two of them over to the wall, where tiny flecks glistened in the light. "Jess, you talk to camera about where we are and then I'll follow the two of you on a walkabout of this level, okay?"

Jess tapped her clip-on microphone and cleared her throat. She waited for Sofia's signal. "We're down here on the digging floor, and you can see, behind me, some of the precious metals—silver as well as gold—still here in the walls. These tiny fragments were often too small to be extracted, so they are left here to add some sparkle to our surroundings. Let's take a walk."

Sofia gave her a thumbs-up before following Jess and Nick as they crept around the digging floor, searching for remains of tools or of the miners themselves. As they approached a corner, Jess pointed, dashing forward and crouching to look at something. Nick and Sofia hurried behind, the camera pointing down through the darkness to reveal a wooden bucket. Rust from the metal handle had eaten through much of the wood surrounding it.

"Should I pick it up?" she said.

Nick bent down to see it, rummaging in his pocket and pulling out a pair of gloves. "Use these," he said. "They're clean. I just don't know if you should handle that rust. Could get a cut or something."

Jess pulled on the gloves and grasped the rounded handle. She tugged it upward, at first stiff against the wood. It creaked and moved, two hunks of rock clattering into one another as it moved. She held it up for the camera to record its crude form.

Sofia sidestepped, capturing the section of wood that was eaten away by rust and mould. The lens darted to the right and behind Jess, to the ground. "Guys, look!" she said, joining them at crouching height.

Nick reached forward, gripping the edge of the paper with care. He brought it up and into the light. His eyes traced the words he could make out in the unmistakeable, faded blue handwriting of the day before.

Another journal entry from his grandfather. "It must've been under the bucket," he said, stepping back into the middle of the chamber. "Sofia, the light from the camera. It's less harsh than my head lamp." He twisted the head torch off, while Sofia steadied the camera.

Jeffrey did not recover from his wound. Robert woke us after discovering the lad not breathing during the night. I tried to find a pulse, but the poor boy was gone. He is with God now, in a better place than this.

And yet, though this place may seem to be some kind of hell, with us watching one of our fellow miners pass before us, still I believe we are not in the absence of the Lord. Last night, an angel visited me, waking me from my sleep and telling me of a place within the mine where we might find freshwater, uncontaminated by the toxins of the ore. It's a quarter mile deeper into the cave. The heat will likely be unbearable, but we shall surely perish without fresh, clean water to drink. I shall ask Robert to accompany me in the morning, once we have found a way to inter young Jeffrey, for Robert is a good man and remains strong.

Nicholas Jones

Sofia reached out for the paper. "Shall I put it into your rucksack?"

Nick shifted it away from her, continued tracing the words. "When do you suppose this was? There's no date. How long would it have taken for Jeffrey to bleed out? How long... How long do you suppose these three men were alive down here?" His eyes passed from Jess to Sofia.

Sofia unzipped the rucksack and reached out towards the paper.

Nick offered it to her this time.

She slipped it into a plastic document sleeve and resealed the bag. "Let's keep going," she said.

CHAPTER SIX

Nick took a single step into the tunnel at the opposite end of the chamber and stopped. He inhaled deeply and turned his head, his torch picking out the uneven textures of the narrow tunnel. He shook his head and stepped backwards.

"Do you want me to go first?" said Jess, close behind.

"I think I'd feel better, yeah." Nick twisted his head lamp off, plunging them into temporary darkness until Jess lit hers. They backed out of the tunnel, changed order and began their descent.

The tunnel's path was steep, dipping at a thirty-degree angle. Jess' light continued to detect nothing but empty space in front of them. After a few minutes, she shuffled herself around, one arm grazing the wall as she rotated in the tight space. "How long is this tunnel on the mine plan?"

Sofia stuffed a hand into Nick's backpack and retrieved the plan. The tunnel was curious: long, narrow, with a wider area in the middle which couldn't be more than ten feet square, then more of the same narrow tunnel for another hundred yards, until the next dig chamber.

"That's weird," said Sofia, her finger hovering over the small space.

Nick moved closer. "Looks like a drop room. Somewhere they could keep heavy tools, or heavily loaded sacks. Easier to have a drop room part way down than to be making trips all the way up to the surface every time."

"Makes sense," Sofia said, getting some still shots of the plan over Nick's shoulder. "Maybe there'll still be some equipment down there." She replaced the plan in Nick's bag and they moved on.

Within a minute the oppressive walls retreated, Nick's breathing shallowed.

Sofia switched on the camera's light, panning across the space. "There," she said, zooming in on a rack of objects in the far corner.

Nick and Jess dashed over, stopping at either side of it.

In the rack stood a long-handled shovel, two pickaxes of varying handle lengths, and a series of chisels. The iron elements of the tools had been badly tarnished by time and humidity. Another bucket stood beside the rack with an oil lamp behind.

"I'm going to get this," said Sofia, coming closer. "Nick, tell us about this equipment."

Nick faced the camera and reached out a hand to the tools. "We've just found this set of tools in this drop room. I suppose we're about a hundred feet below the surface now. Here we've got chisels of different shapes and sizes, used for more detailed work. They would have had hammers, too, but I can't see any of them here. The pickaxes, here, would be used for the initial breaking of the rock face, while this shovel would be used to fill the buckets over there with nuggets or chunks of rock that were likely to have a large gold contingent."

Sofia gave a thumbs-up and lowered the camera. "Perfect," she said.

Jess stood, handling the shorter of the two picks, eyes wide. "Um, guys... I'm not sure this is just rust." She moved the linear cutting blade at the rear into the light, a reddish-brown tarnish, tinged with green, spread across it like perversely twisted fingers.

Nick twisted on his head torch, illuminating it more clearly. He reached down for the larger pickaxe and brought it into the light. It, too, bore a terracotta-coloured stain, but it was dotted at irregular intervals across the entire iron surface and absent of the green.

"Turn it over," Nick said, replacing the larger axe.

Jess flipped it, casting the wooden handle into the light. The blood was clear to see now, soaked into the grain of the light wood beneath the iron.

"This is the one. This must have been the one that my grandfather used...on Jeffrey's hand." He wrung his hands in front of him, his eyes wandered. "They must have come this way. After the initial collapse. We're getting closer to...to the remains."

Jess placed the pickaxe back into the rack.

"Let's see if this works, shall we?" She lifted the oil lamp from the ground, a pleasant sloshing of the liquid inside echoing from the nearby walls. Sofia handed her camera to Nick, placed her rucksack on the ground, and took out a packet of matches, handing them to Jess. Jess struck a match, lifted the glass tube, and held the flame over the desiccated wick. It flickered, sparked, then lit. She turned the small metal dial at one side and heard fuel flowing, causing the flame to grow. "Perfect."

The light from the lamp was warmer, more golden than the cold, white halogens of the head torches. "Let's use this for a while. Save batteries. What do you think?" said Nick.

Jess made an affirmative murmur and twisted off her head lamp. "Do you want to lead us through the next stretch?" she said, offering Nick the lamp.

He stepped back, hands raised, and inhaled deeply. "I do not. After you." He gestured towards the downward tunnel and fell in line behind her as she entered.

They had taken no more than five steps down when the ground beneath them began to shake. A low-pitched rumble, louder than before, hummed in their rib cages.

Jess spun in spite of the tight space, thrusting the lantern almost into Nick's chin, before lowering it to waist-height. "Let's move back into the drop room. There's more space."

Nick tried to speak, but air refused to enter his lungs. His voice came out a terrified, wordless whisper. He nodded and stepped back, glancing back to be sure Sofia wasn't too close. They edged out of the tunnel and into the wider space.

Jess searched Nick's face. "You okay?"

His skin was slicked with sweat, his lower lip quivering. The quaking ground stilled. "I think I'm... I think I need to sit down." He looked about the chamber, then Sofia pointed to an outcrop of stone, jutting from the wall. He staggered over, his legs almost failing him, and lowered himself into a sitting position. He wiped at the sweat with the back of his forearm. "I'm okay. Thanks. Thank you." He looked from Sofia to Jess who was peering up into the tunnel which led to ground level.

"What is it?" Sofia's voice, too, was inflected with fear. "Al said the hydraulics should be able to withstand these tremors, right? *Right?*"

Nick didn't respond. His lips moved, forming unspoken words, his eyes unable to focus.

Jess lowered the lamp to the ground, eyes still fixed on the tunnel. She stood to her full height, then twisted on the head torch on her helmet. "I just want to check the entrance. Just in case." She didn't wait for a reply, her quick feet disappearing up and into the darkness, the sound of her hurried footsteps swallowed seconds later.

Minutes passed and the silence grew, until the sound of the flame consuming oil as it bled through the wick of the lamp seemed to rise to a roar.

Sofia stood. "I'm going to see if she's oka—"

"We're *fucked*!" Jess' voice from some distant part of the tunnel. A minute or so later, she re-entered the chamber, coughing as the dust kicked up by the cave-in invaded her lungs. "The entrance has collapsed."

CHAPTER SEVEN

Sofia sat, noticing Nick's face as the colour faded from it. Nick closed his eyes. He crouched, his back against the wall, his hands together as though in prayer, covering his mouth and nose. His eyes opened, darting back and forth between the darkness of the tunnel and Jess, phone aloft, keenly focussed on the screen for any sign of reception.

"How far back from the entrance are we?" She glared at Nick, then at Sofia, as the question hung in the air. "Why won't this fucking thing work?" She began to pace again, her arm outstretched towards the tunnel ceiling, above, hand clutching the phone.

"Jess, stop." Sofia placed her hands on Jess' shoulders. "Look." She nodded over Jess' shoulder to a wooden bracket on the wall, holding back several small boulders, a few yards back from the limit of the cave-in. "That bracket was a long way from the entrance. And this rock is metal-rich. It's going to interfere with reception."

Jess sniffed, blinked her eyes, and nodded, lowering her arm and depositing the phone into the pocket of her shorts. "Thanks," she said. "Nick, do you want to try the satellite phone?"

Nick stood, gathering up his rucksack and began rummaging in one of the inside pockets. "James said this would work down to about a hundred and fifty feet of depth, so we shouldn't have any problem here." He pulled out the bulky, rubberised device and pressed the power button. It buzzed in his hand until the old-fashioned green screen illuminated. He paused for a few moments, waiting for it to find the satellite signal, until the LCD screen announced it was '*ready.*'

Jess read James' number to him, and he dialled. Waited. A woman's voice answered. "Hi, it's Nick. Nick Jones, from the mine site up near Mariposa. I need to speak to James. It's urgent."

The woman at the other end of the phone took a deep breath, released it. "Mr. Greene is in a meeting with investors at the moment. Can you call back in an hour or so, or can I take a message?"

Nick made a sound somewhere between a dry laugh and a cough and wiped the sweat from his forehead with his free hand. "I cannot call back in an hour, because we have just been buried by an earthquake in a mine, while making Mr. Greene's show. I'm sorry about the investors, but I need to speak to him *right now.*"

Sofia stared, wide-eyed, at Nick.

He shrugged his shoulders and flashed her a smile.

The phone crackled. "Nick, Lorraine's just told me. What do you need me to do?"

"James, hi. Look, the entrance has caved in. There doesn't seem to be any structural damage deeper down, but we're going to need Al's team here to dig us out."

He heard the scratching of a pencil on the other end of the phone. "Got that. Look, Nick…it's after four already. We're going to have to face the possibility of you guys spending the night down there. I'm gonna call Al right away and get him to come back to you on this number with advice. Can you stay put, exactly where you are, and keep the sat phone connected?"

Nick nodded his head. "Yes. Yeah, of course."

"Al'll be through to you within the half hour."

The line cut out. Nick lowered the phone, his eyes lingering on the LCD as the green light faded.

"So?" Jess was pacing again.

"We wait. He said Al would call within half an hour."

"And he'll dig us out?"

"Of course he'll dig us out but...look... James said we need to be aware of the time. If Al's team isn't here until after five." Nick looked at his watch, then back at Jess. "We might have to face sleeping down here tonight."

Jess ruffled her hair, eyes closed. "I don't fucking believe—"

Sofia raised a hand, cutting her off. "Look, guys. Let's sit. Save our energy. If we're going to be down here a while, we just have to make the best of it." She sat on an even patch of ground and gestured for the two of them to join her.

Jess chewed on her bottom lip for a moment before sitting.

Sofia sipped from her water flask, then offered it over to Jess. "So, Nick, don't take this the wrong way, but you don't seem like a guy who's always wanted to come down a mine."

Nick took the flask and drank a few mouthfuls before handing it back to Sofia. "The claustrophobia *is* pretty bad. Fucking earthquakes don't help, though."

They all laughed quietly.

"Really, though, I read about you. You were doing great as an academic. Why are you here? *So* far outside your comfort zone."

He rested against the wall, looking for an answer. "When I was growing up, my grandad was my hero. This story...the story of this place...was more important to me than all the Greek myths, all the fairy tales. My grandad, the *real* saviour of men, against all the odds. All that, you know?" He picked up a small piece of rock, turned it over in front of his face, then threw it into the dark tunnel. "Anyway, when

I began to get older, I started to understand things differently. People's ideas...opinions. When my dad ran out on us...I must have been ten, eleven, I suppose. I started to see then. People...those small-town folk...they started to say my mum...she'd chosen badly. Chosen a rogue. Same as her mum." Nick closed his eyes, whispered. "Same as her mum."

Sofia stuffed the flask into her sack, packing her camera away on top. "Did you start to have doubts? About him, I mean?"

Nick fixed Sofia with his stare, his eyes wet. "Never. I just knew that, one day, I'd get here. I'd prove them all wrong."

Sofia nodded, reached out to touch Jess on the shoulder. "You okay?"

A clang sounded from deep in the mine before she could reply—a single sound, metal against metal, echoing from far below. The three of them glanced at one another, eyes searching for meaning.

Again the sound came, striking twice now, echoes bleeding from one sound into the other.

"Knockers," Jess said under her breath.

"Excuse me?" Sofia cocked her head.

Another sound, this one deeper, booming. Like a great stone body colliding with another. The earth seemed to tremble, somehow differently than during the quake. Momentary, localised. Then everything went still.

A buzz in the centre of the room, and the sat phone bleeped. Nick picked up. "Al, is that you?"

The low growl of machinery distorted the sound from the phone. "We're just coming to Mariposa now. Should be with you in about fifteen minutes. Nick, I need you guys to stay back from the entryway. Maybe down into the second chamber, a bit lower. We need to use a radar device and your physical bodies can skew the results. Can you do that for me? Safely, I mean."

"We're on the mid-level, in the first drop room. I think we'll be safe."

"No problem. I'll call back in half an hour with a plan and some timescales." The phone clicked off.

"So?" Jess was already scrambling to her feet.

"We need to stay down here while they assess the entrance." Nick laid back on the ground.

Sofia lowered herself onto her back, beside him. "What are the knockers?" she said.

"A fairy tale," Nick said.

CHAPTER EIGHT

"This must be what it's like to be in a bomb shelter," Jess said in a period of calm amongst the rumbling from above. "Except the danger is down here and safety..." Her eyes rolled towards the ceiling and particles of dense earth that drifted like umber snow towards the floor. "Safety is out there."

Nick stood, then adjusted his stance as he felt the closeness of the ceiling. He began pacing in the small space, the flickering light of the lantern animating his shadow on the far wall. "There's no danger down here. Not as long as they can get us out."

"Even then, it's only *slow* danger. Thirst. Starvation. Suffocation." Sofia held Nick's gaze as she spoke. "My God, Nick, your grandpa. I'm sorry."

"It's okay. I know you didn't mean to..."

Sofia went on. "You spoke to Al, right at the beginning. You know he's a professional. We'll be in my trailer with a glass of wine in a few hours, laughing about this."

Nick crouched, forced a smile onto his face. "You're right. I'm sure you're right."

The sound of drilling filled the air as the machines bored into the rock face. Nick felt sweat trace a path down the back of his neck and under his shirt as his eyes moved from one wall of the tiny chamber to the other. He tightened the muscles in his cheeks back into a grin, then lowered his head, counting fives as he breathed in and out, eyes closed.

A violent, distant crash rang out, seeming to move the very air. The three looked at one another, Jess' lips parted, ready to say something but not knowing quite what.

A beep emanated from the sat phone.

"Al, is that you?" Nick said.

"Nick, it's me. We've cleared a path for you all to exit the mine. My guys have looked at the cave-in. There are some…unusual signs here. Anyway, my advice is to get out as quickly as you can. How deep are you?"

"We're not that deep. We're halfway to the second mining floor. About a hundred and fifty feet if I remember. What are these signs you mentioned?"

"It's best if you see it for yourself. Just hurry, okay?"

Headlights from the heavy machinery cast Al's shadow far across the rubble-strewn ground as he crouched in the entrance. His big right hand was clutching something shiny, but it was difficult to make it out through the glare of the bright lights. Nick shielded his eyes with his hands and stooped. The hydraulic support that Al was clutching was punctured, liquid pooled around scattered chunks of rock.

Nick scanned the section of metal around the puncture, absorbing the detail of the torn, twisted material. "How much pressure would it take to create a puncture like this?"

"None," said Al, standing. "I had two of my guys look at it, and they agree with me. This isn't strain damage. This is from an impact. Something sharp hit it with a lot of force."

Nick stood, nodded to Jess and Sofia as they arrived. He tugged at a handful of his hair, his eyes locked on the broken support. "It could have been a rock with a sharp edge, flung by the tremor."

"Could've been, sure," said Al. "But, with all your mining knowledge, how likely would you say that is?"

Nick felt Sofia and Jess' eyes burning into the side of his head as he thought about an answer. His eyes darted from the debris on the ground to the boulders layering the walls around them. "I'd say it's almost impossible."

Al kicked the support, sending it sliding across the uneven ground, drops of amber liquid spurting up and landing on his work boots. "So, we're in agreement."

"Wait a minute." Jess stepped forward as she spoke, her hand raised, palm-forward towards Al. "If that explanation is *impossible*, what the hell *did* happen to this thing?"

Nick shrugged. "There's no way of knowing for su—"

"But what do you *think* happened? What would be your guess, based on the evidence we have?" Jess' nose almost touched Nick's chin as she glared up at him.

Nick took a step back, swallowed. "If I saw this…" He gestured down to the broken support rod. "On an inspection, for example, I'd assume… I would assume sabotage."

"But we were the only ones down here," Jess said.

The men's eyes met, but no words were exchanged for a long moment.

Sofia placed a calming hand on Jess' shoulder. "Let's all just get outside to the trailers, shall we?"

She guided them both beyond Al and out, into the night. At the trailer door Sofia directed Jess to the table, before opening the small freezer compartment in the fridge and taking out a slim glass bottle without a label. She poured three fingers of the almost-clear liquid into each of two glasses and pushed one across to Jess.

"Tequila," she said. "We need it."

Jess lifted her glass, angling her head to look at the volume inside. "Sofia, this shot is huge!"

Sofia reached out with her hand, blocking Jess' arm before she downed the drink. "This is good stuff. It's for sipping. Not like that shit you throw down your neck in England."

The words were parcelled in a playful smile that Jess returned. She took a sip and seemed to relax immediately. She placed the glass back onto the table and took one of Sofia's hands in her own. "Thank you for this." She slouched back in her seat, clearly struggling to keep her eyes open.

Nick remained in the doorway, his hands together in front of him. "I think we should get some rest." he said,

"Tequila first, then rest," said Sofia. "Have some." She stood and reached up to the compact cupboard above the table for another glass.

Nick crossed his arms and shook his head. "No, thank you. Not tonight. I'll see you both in the morning." He walked slowly over to his own trailer and sat on the step, watching as the two beads of glowing red light that were the taillights of Al's struck snaked down the hillside. Constellations of small towns twinkled in the moonless darkness.

Once the truck was out of sight, he stood, pulled the lever on the door, and went inside, closing it behind him. As he lay down, unsure whether it was real or a dream, he heard the distant, rhythmic clang of metal on metal.

CHAPTER NINE

Scant light crept in beneath the curtains of the trailer as the noise of the trucks shook Nick from his sleep. He looked at his watch. Almost seven in the morning. The sun rose from behind the mountain range above them. The dark lingered in that place. He stretched and pulled on some shorts, then ambled to the kitchenette. He spooned coffee into the stove top coffee maker and turned on the gas, his eyes glued to the flame for a while as he thought about the tremor. The broken support rod. The pierced cylinder that looked...*deliberate* was the only word he could come up with. He rubbed a hand across his forehead and down to his cheeks, his eyes scrunched shut, then reached up to the overhead cupboard for a mug. A writhing tendril of coffee-scented steam rose from the spout.

Nick opened the door of his trailer, allowing morning air in, cold and bracing. He immediately felt more awake. Incredible, the contrast between the baking days and the chill of the night and early morning. He poked his head around the corner and watched as Al and two of his workmen moved debris from the mine entrance, seven or eight gleaming new pieces of support apparatus awaiting installation on a trailer behind Al's truck. The cold air suddenly bit at Nick's bare torso, so he moved back inside and turned off the fire under the bubbling coffee pot.

He poured a liberal splash of creamer into his mug and then drowned it with coffee, watching the two liquids swirl together in a one-sided fight for supremacy. Scalding hot, the liquid burned his mouth, but something close to humanity rushed back into his sleep-addled mind. He took down another mug and filled it with coffee. After putting on a thin shirt, and flip flops, Nick stepped down from the door to the dusty ground.

Placing one of the cups down on the ground, he rapped on the door of Jess' trailer. His gaze was drawn up the hill to the mine entrance, as the two men lugged the supports one at a time on some kind of trolley while Al gesticulated wildly, directing them. He stepped back and knocked on the door again, a little harder this time.

"Nick," came a voice from behind and to his left. Jess stood in the doorway of Sofia's trailer, wearing a t-shirt and shivering in the cold morning air.

He bent down to pick up the mug, held it out towards her. "I made us some coffee," he said, annoyed with himself that he was feeling so sheepish.

"Where's mine?" Sofia's voice found its way from the trailer into the windy air. She appeared from behind Jess, also in a t-shirt, her legs a shade darker than Jess' in front. She smiled broadly, then planted a kiss into the messy nest of Jess' hair.

Nick stumbled forward awkwardly, handing the first mug to Jess. "There's more in the pot," he said and half jogged back to the trailer to find another mug. Coffee sloshed around as he walked back across the makeshift campsite, past the blackened fire pit from the first night. He stepped up into the trailer to find the two women sat at the table, both wearing knee-length shorts now, with bowls of granola and yogurt with berries. "Here," he said, handing the steaming mug across to Sofia.

She took it and glugged some of it down. "Mmm...thanks, Nick. Stay for breakfast. I brought these strawberries with me. They're delicious."

Nick glanced over at Jess, who nodded and offered him a warm smile, patting the bench beside her. Nick sat and reached for a bowl.

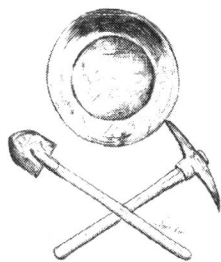

With breakfast done, they each returned to their own trailers to get fully dressed and prepped for the day. Fifteen minutes later, they stood at the mouth of the mine, the stillness amplifying the sound of the stones rolling under their feet.

Al's men sat in the furthest of two trucks. Al leaned into the window, talking over some final details. He stepped back, tapped his hand on the bonnet, and they drove off, a trail of dust drifting away on the breeze. "The boys have more than doubled the number of struts supporting the ground level," Al said as he walked back to the group. "In theory, it should be way more than what's required for the structure of the shaft. But...as we saw yesterday..."

Nick looked across to Sofia, then to Jess. "Understood, Al. Thanks for doing this," he said, shaking his hand. "We've got five days left on the original filming schedule. As we've had no message to say otherwise, we have to assume that's our remaining time frame."

"If the mine entrance holds, that should be more than possible," said Sofia.

"Right then," Nick said. "Let's check our packs one last time and get down there."

Nick lowered his rucksack from his back and began to run through the mental list of everything he could need. Jess and Sofia followed suit.

Al climbed into his truck and started the engine. "Hey, Nick!" he called out over the rumble. "The number I called from…to the sat phone. It's my personal cell number. If anything happens… It shouldn't, but…you know?"

Nick nodded. "You'll be the first to know."

They watched as the truck disappeared along the winding mountain roads, then turned to the mine entrance, shiny support struts standing like gleaming sentinels in the midst of the dark.

"Almost ten," said Sofia, checking her watch. She squeezed the handle of the camera with her right hand. "Let's go."

CHAPTER TEN

"What *is* that smell?" Jess covered her mouth and nose with her hands as her eyes traced the lines of the new chamber, illuminated by the lantern's flickering light.

Nick stopped beside her, wincing. "I don't know. It smells like...like..."

"Like an animal," Sofia said before he could finish. The camera was on her shoulder as they entered the new layer of the mine, night vision filters kicking in as the scale of the place seemed to soak up the light.

"You think something died down here?" Jess' hand muffled her voice.

"Uh-uh," said Sofia, panning with her camera to inspect every corner of the cavernous chamber. "I know that smell from when I used to visit my *Tio* across the border. That's something *alive*."

Nick took the lantern from Jess and paced deeper into the space, the light ghosting him like a warm halo. Sofia followed with the camera, using the lantern light to pick out details on the far wall.

"There's nothing here," said Nick, turning and striding back across to them.

"But there was." Sofia lowered the camera, the red recording light no longer on.

"Well, we don't kno—"

"You don't smell that?" Her eyes were alive with energy. "*Something* was in this chamber. Not long before we arrived. Could've been a bear, a coyote... I don't know. We need to be super careful."

Nick held up his hands in a disarming gesture. "Okay, okay. We'll be *extremely* careful. No one wants any of us to get hurt down here." He reached into his pack and pulled out the sat phone, handing it to Sofia. "You're at the back. If you see something, dial the emergency number, right away."

Sofia nodded, seeming content for now.

"Let's shoot some to-camera stuff here, then search the area more thoroughly," she said, lifting the camera to her shoulder and starting it rolling again. She moved in towards Nick, fragments of metal glinting along the walls.

Nick smoothed down his shirt and took a breath. "This chamber here is huge. The map we recovered from the archives showed this room at...maybe forty percent of this size. It's a mining floor, open-faced on at least two of the sides." He gestured to the uneven wall to his right, chunks of rock clearly cut away, leaving it uneven, jagged. "Let's take a look on the ground, see if we can find any other tools or anything like that."

He began to walk along the side wall, the lantern out in front, scouring the rocky ground for any sign of something left behind. "Anything over that side, Jess?" he called, his voice echoing.

There was no reply.

"Jess?" he shouted again.

"*Jess?*" Sofia called with greater urgency. She panned with her camera to the other side of the chamber and focussed on Jess crouched, close to the ground.

"Guys," she said finally. "Guys, I think you'd better see this."

Nick paced across the chamber as fast as he could without upturning the lantern, its light immediately revealing another sheet of ragged journal paper. "Is it...from my grandfather?"

Jess nodded her head.

Nick crouched beside her, the light illuminating her face and revealing that she was biting her lip now, a single tear tracing a path down her cheek before falling to the ground.

"What is it? What does it say?" said Sofia, camera still recording.

Jess scooped up the paper and held it to her chest. "I...I don't think you should see it." She was looking intently into Nick's eyes as she spoke.

"What the hell do you mean?" he said, reaching for the paper.

"I'm serious. No. It's not good. It's not *normal*."

Nick reached in for it again, his finger and thumb gripping the corner. He pulled at it and stopped as it began to tear. "Of course it's not normal. He was a man dying in a mine. With no hope. God knows how long he'd been down here by the time he—"

"Nick," She shouted his name, despite their proximity, then sniffed, closing her eyes. "You don't want to read it. Trust me."

"I have to." Nick reached forward and took hold of the paper.

This time Jess released her grip. "Wait! Turn that off." She pointed at Sofia's camera.

Nick squeezed Jess' arm. "I don't think it's nec—"

"Turn it off. Read it and then decide." Jess shoved Nick's hand away and slumped to the ground.

Today is May 19th.

It is the third day since we finished our rations. Daniel, the remaining American, is sickly and weak. Robert is making his best efforts to hide the effects of hunger, but I have noticed the anguish in his eyes. I have felt it myself as hunger pangs knot my stomach.

So it was then, during the night, the angel came to me once more. I blessed him for his guidance in finding the water, as the three of us would surely otherwise have expired already. He told me I must remain strong, that I must keep my faith. That I must eat. We all must.

He instructed me to find the place where we had interred Jeffrey and to disturb his shallow grave. That the meat from his body might sustain us. I was shocked. Horrified, even. I begged the angel's forgiveness for doubting him as I asked him whether cannibalism were not after all an unholy act.

The angel placed his hand upon mine, and I felt the coolness of his skin there, calming me. While to eat the flesh of your fellow man was indeed wrong in the eyes of God, he told me that to allow three further souls to be extinguished was a sin far greater.

I told Robert and Daniel of his visit in the morning, though they seemed not to understand. They were incredulous that I would consider such a deed. I reminded them of the water source which my angel had led us to, but they still refused to heed my words.

Thus, to keep us all alive, I shall return to the grave this night. I shall follow the angel's instructions.

And we shall eat. We shall survive. In God's name, we shall survive.

Nicholas Jones

Nick stood and left the chamber the way they had entered. Jess scrambled to her feet and called after him. He didn't respond. The sound of his footsteps reverberated around the chamber for a few moments and then all was silent.

Sofia held the paper in the lantern light as he left, reading it a second time. "He'll come back," she said. "He'll be okay."

CHAPTER ELEVEN

The darkness grew impenetrable before Nick realised he had left the lantern behind in the other room. In his mind's eye, images of his grandfather flashed before him, the charming smile he'd looked upon with such wonder throughout his youth, tinged with a single droplet of crimson descending from his pursed lips.

He stumbled on an indentation in the rocky mine floor, almost losing his balance, and switched on his head torch. His pulse thumped in his ears, breath short and heavy. He stopped just before climbing the final slope to the entrance and slid down the wall.

"Why the fuck am I even here?" he said aloud. "What am I trying to prove? Fuck's sake."

He chewed on his lip and felt tears well in his eyes. Blinking them away, he cleared his throat. The echo of his cough subsided, and all that was left was the sound of his own nervous breathing. He reached his hand to his chest, the rise and fall shallower now. He inhaled, held it.

With his own breath silenced, it was undeniable. The unmistakable sound of someone panting.

Not him.

"Hello?" he said, turning his head one way and then the other, the light from his head torch casting shadows over the craggy walls. "Jess? Sofia?"

Then a sound from above him, rock crumbling, movement.

His vision darted up, the cone of light following close behind. But there was no one. Nothing.

"Hey!" he called again, then quieted himself until the echo passed.

There was no sound, no breathing, just blood drumming blast-beats in his temples. Nick scrambled to his feet and hurried back to where he'd left the girls.

CHAPTER TWELVE

"Are you sure you're okay to continue?" Jess stood face to face with Nick, her fingers making circles on his upper arms.

Nick was trembling despite the warm, clammy atmosphere at that depth. He nodded his head. "I just...spooked myself. After reading that letter, you know? It's nothing. Besides, time is against us."

Sofia stood and moved towards the mouth of the tunnel at the end of the large chamber they were in. "I'll lead for a while," she said, and twisted on her head torch to pierce the veil of dark in front of her.

Jess held the lantern to one side, casting Nick's shadow long and angular across the walls.

Nick watched as Sofia entered the tunnel, her form becoming less distinct until she was nothing more than a willowy silhouette. He lengthened his strides to catch up with her and quickly found himself frozen, suddenly aware of the oppressive proximity of the walls. They seemed to close in further as he glanced around. He coughed. Began wheezing. He reached a hand out to support himself on the wall. The cold earth appeared to draw out what little warmth was left in his body. His ears began to ring and then he was falling, his eyes tricking him, as though he was watching someone else fall. He clattered to the ground and the darkness turned a shade blacker.

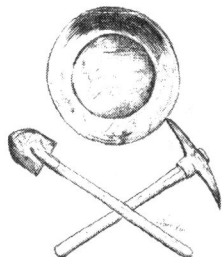

Cool water ran over his face. Nick instinctively scrunched his eyes shut and turned his head.

Jess stroked his forehead with her right hand, her left supporting him. "Nick. You blacked out."

His eyes peeled open, as though glued shut. He stared up into Jess' face, glowing in the light of the lantern. "He ate them," Nick said.

"Who ate who? What are you talking about?" Jess lowered his head gently to the ground, then she stood, pulling her arms tightly around herself, as though feeling the phantom chill which had gripped Nick before his fall. "Your grandfather? Jeffrey? The boy was dead, Nick. In circumstances like these, cannibalism is more common than you might think."

"Let's get him to his feet, shall we?" Sofia crouched, locking an arm under one of Nick's. "Do you think you can stand?"

Nick nodded his head, mumbling, before the two women elevated him until his feet pressed firmly against the floor of the tunnel. "How far..?"

"It's about fifteen yards to the next section of the mine. The floor level drops a bit. Watch out for it. Then we can take a moment, make sure you haven't bumped that head of yours." Sofia's words reverberated off the walls as she led the way forward.

No one spoke; all focussed on feeling for the slope ahead. The incline was sudden, steep. Nick propped himself up against the wall with his shoulder, still feeling somewhat off-balance. Jess, behind him, kept one hand out in front, ready to grab him if he slipped or fell. Then they were out into a new expanse, the echo of the rocks moving under foot telling them that this one was big.

"Wow," said Jess, her voice rebounding from walls and ceiling and cracks in the rock and returning to her over and over. "This place must be huge!" She raised the lantern, sweeping an arc in front of her without finding any wall ahead. "Even the ceiling is way up."

Everyone turned their eyes upward, unable to pierce through the murk to the top. Nick lowered his pack to the ground and sat on it. He pulled the laminated plan of the mine from the side pocket and unfolded it. "This is it, guys. The heart of the mine. According to the drawings and the ground radar, this space is more than two thousand cubic feet, with some natural cave structures…pockets really, about thirty feet up."

"Judging from the drawing on the note your grandfather left, this is also close to the water source that his *angel* told him about. Can I take another look at it?" Sofia outstretched her hand, turning her head from side to side, scouring the walls for tunnel entrances with the brilliant light of her head torch.

Nick thrust his hand into the waterproof document pocket inside his pack and pulled out the small sheaf of papers. He carefully unfolded the sheets until he found the note with the hand-drawn map, then handed it over.

Sofia scanned it, pacing the width of the space they were in, her eyes keenly darting from the paper to her surroundings and back again. "Here," Sofia called.

Jess lowered the lantern to the ground, then dashed towards her. "Are you sure?" Jess scrutinised the drawing with only Sofia's head torch to illuminate it. "Isn't this the tunnel we came in th—"

"Shh... Listen. Do you hear that?" Sofia cocked her head, listening intently. "It sounds like moving water. My God."

"We should take a look. Nick, do you want to stay here? Catch your breath?" Jess asked, skipping back to grab the lantern and leaving it beside him. "Are you feeling a little better?"

Nick took the water bottle and drank a long swallow. "I'm completely fine. Go and check out the water. But be careful."

"Of course," Jess said, already halfway to the exit tunnel.

CHAPTER THIRTEEN

Sofia led the way along the tunnel while Jess twisted the dial of her own head torch to off. The path was wider than the one they'd come in by and the rushing sound was growing, magnified as it bounced off the walls. The sounds of their footsteps, and of the stones slipping underfoot were drowned out by it until they were imperceptible.

"What does it mean?" said Jess, the light from her torch bobbing with her strides.

"What does *what* mean?" Sofia's tone was harsh, bristling.

Jess remained silent for a few moments, mulling over whether or not to elaborate. "The water," she finally managed. "If there is running water—*clean* water—what does that mean about Nick's grandpa's story?"

Sofia sighed deeply. She paced a few steps then stopped. "It means he was right about the water."

"Nothing more? What about the angel?"

Sofia chuckled and turned to face Jess. "Are you serious? An angel? You have to be kidding!"

Jess folded her arms. "How else would he know about the water source?" She felt herself pouting, detected the spikiness in her own voice. "I'm sorry... But don't you think it's a little odd?"

Sofia brought her right hand up to her chin and grinned. "You're serious, aren't you?" She laughed again, deeper in her belly this time. "Do you know how long men spent in the mines in the fifties? He'd been here a little over two months, but I bet he'd been spending close to twelve hours a day down here. If that was you...you and your buddies...you wouldn't see your way to exploring the places that were off the map?"

Jess shrugged, chewing at her bottom lip.

"I think he'd come across the water source—*if* there is one—before, and then...after the cave-in... Well, you can't blame the guy for hallucinations." Sofia turned and paced towards the sound once more.

Jess hadn't moved. "You don't believe in angels?"

Sofia froze. Spun around. The blaring light at a distance cast their shadows long, face to face, superimposed upon halos of gold. "That's a different question."

"So...what's the answer?" Jess stood her ground. Felt her breathing quicken a little.

Sofia took a step closer, the line of her nose and the tips of her spiky hair painting detail onto her silhouette. "I grew up in a Catholic household. My parents are Mexican, but you knew that already." She kicked at a stone on the ground and folded one hand around the fingers of the other. "When that all... When it falls apart, you question things."

"Your family?"

"Exactly, but more than that. Some of the places I've travelled to. The things I've seen. Kids running drugs, sometimes even forced into selling their bodies—sometimes both… I didn't see any angels in those places. Places where people most needed one."

Jess moved closer, reaching out with one hand and knitting her fingers with Sofia's. "You don't believe anymore."

"I didn't say that," Sofia said and tugged Jess' hand, bringing her closer to her. She raised her hand and kissed her palm. "I believe in the dark. Evil. You can't see the things I have and dismiss that. And if there's evil…real darkness…"

"There has to be some light somewhere?"

Sofia nodded. "I hope for that, at least." She slipped an arm around Jess' back, her fingers tracing the indentations of her lean muscles. "And what about you? Do you believe there's an angel down here? Or that there was? Do you believe they exist?"

Jess edged nearer, feeling the sweat on her forearms meld with that of Sofia's shoulder. "I'm British. We don't really do religion. But I try to keep an open mind." She lowered her head, her lips grazing Sofia's cheek and then finding her mouth. She kissed her softly and allowed her eyes to close, focusing on the lines of Sofia's body as they fit against hers.

Sofia twisted her neck, breaking the embrace.

"What is it?" Jess' cheeks burned as she spoke.

"I'm still worried about Nick. We should check for the water, shoot a sequence if we find it, and get back to him."

Jess' blush spread to her neck and beyond. "Of course. I'm sorry."

"Don't be," said Sofia and took one final taste of Jess' mouth. "Later." She turned her back and hurried on, Jess following close behind this time. Within a few moments, the swaying arc of her light caught the beginning of a widening path. "There," she said, her steps quickening into a jog.

Jess kept pace with her until they stepped into a cavernous space with a low, undulating ceiling. Water flowed down the rear wall and into an angular pool.

Sofia ducked low and sidestepped towards the water's edge. "See how fast it's running? But it doesn't overflow. Must be an underground reservoir or something." She lowered her pack to the ground and unfastened her camera holster, setting it beside the bag. She unbuttoned her overshirt and laid it on top of the pack.

"What are you doing?" said Jess, struggling to keep her eyes from the tight vest Sofia was wearing.

Sofia lowered herself on to her side and crawled to the water's edge. "I'm trying to see if I can reach the bottom." She lunged down with her right arm and moved it around, leaning on her left, her brow fixed with concentration. She pulled the arm back out. "Can't feel anything. There must be gallons of what looks like fresh water down there. Incredible." She scrambled to her feet, shaking her wet hand to remove the excess water, then reached for her camera. "Get over here, we should shoot a segment here, then we'll put some of this water in one of my flasks. We can send it for testing on the surface. See if it's drinkable."

Jess lowered her pack to the ground and crept closer, peering in and watching as the end of her head torch beam disappeared into the depths. She twisted the torch off as she turned to Sofia. "You absolutely *have* to put that shirt back on if you want me to concentrate."

Sofia's cheeks flushed as she pulled on the shirt and buttoned it almost to the top. She held up her camera, shifted the focus until Jess was crystal clear in front of her. "Okay, we're good to go."

"This is day four and we are in the deepest part of the mine that we've been able to explore so far. We've followed the sound of running water along a series of tunnels and have found what looks like a spring and, from first appearances, it does *not* seem to be contaminated." She crouched down and scooped up some water, allowing it to cascade from one hand into the other before splashing to the ground. "What makes this find particularly interesting is that in Nicholas Jones' journal pages, found inside the mine by our very own Nick two days ago, he mentions a water source, pointed out to him by an angel after the original collapse. Subsequent journal pages reveal that he and his co-workers did manage to survive for several days, meaning it's fairly likely they did indeed use this water source here to quench their thirst."

"And cut there." Sofia tilted the camera forward, watching the footage back on the LCD screen. "It looks great, especially considering the low light in here." She lowered the camera back into its holster and hauled her pack onto her back. She pulled the smaller of two flasks from a side pocket and drained what little water remained in a single swallow, then dunked it down into the water until it was half full. "Now, let's go see if our Welshman is feeling any better, shall we?"

Jess nodded and led the way out of the chamber and back into the tunnel. "Sofia, do you think I said too much? Bringing up the notes?"

Sofia placed a hand on Jess' shoulder and squeezed. "The very reason we're here is to tell the older Nicholas Jones' story. It just seems the story is a little longer—and way more terrifying—than any of us had anticipated."

CHAPTER FOURTEEN

Nick listened to the footsteps die down to silence before he stood up. Every time he blinked, he saw the image—like a dream—of his grandfather and the other men, slicing meat from the fallen American boy. He lifted the lantern from the floor and headed to the far wall, just beyond the tunnel the girls had disappeared into. Flecks of gold and other metals glistened in the light from the lantern as he walked the length of the chamber.

So huge was the space, and so quiet, the shuffling of his feet was a cacophony. The crunch of stones and long untouched soil underfoot crashing off the walls and ceiling before hurtling back to him and assaulting him again.

He stopped. Listened to the sound reverberate around the chamber until it fell silent.

Another crunch. Above.

He lifted the lantern. Narrowed his eyes, trying to make out any shape. Anything *moving*.

Nothing.

He stamped his foot hard on the ground. A boom like thunder echoed around, flying back to him four times over and then dying. Silence was restored.

Then something moved. High above him, at the very limit of the lantern's light. With his free hand, he twisted on the head torch and scanned one way and then the next. No sign of any animal, nor any movement. He stepped back, panning with his head again. A flash. Something bright, metallic. Then a shadow, moving to his right.

He flicked his head, squinted. Only darkness.

His heart thumped in his chest. Reaching into his bag, he pulled out a distress flare. He pulled the ignition strip and the walls were immediately painted a vivid red. Nick held the flare at arm's length, turning his head slightly to avoid the noxious smoke that spewed lazily from the seal at the top.

He turned back to the metallic something his keen eyes had found. Two of them now, maybe more, glinting in the red light from the flare. Small, fine. Impossible to make out their shape from here. They were suspended, above ledges of sorts, high above the ground. There was no way up there.

He would stand and watch for movement. He would be brave. Not let the terror, infiltrating his mind and body more with every passing moment, win. Waiting for the others and hoping the flare didn't sputter out before they returned.

CHAPTER FIFTEEN

"Nick!" Jess called out as they neared the exit of the tunnel. "There's water! Free flowing water, just like the note said."

Sofia emerged from the shadow with Jess close behind, their features being filled in, as though by a sketch artist, the closer they came to the flare.

Nick held his position, glancing from the high walls of the chamber to the girls and back again. "That's...that's amazing. Do...you think it's drinkable?" Nick's voice wavered as he spoke, his terse expression giving away that something wasn't quite right.

Sofia gazed up towards the ceiling. "It was crystal clear, so I think there's a good chance it's uncontaminated." She squinted her eyes. "What the hell are you looking at?" As she spoke, the flare faded to a pale pink before dying and leaving them in the dimmer lantern light.

Nick bent his knees, so that his height approximated Sofia's, then pointed. "Do you see that? Follow my index finger. Something…metallic, it looks like."

Sofia swiped at his hand. "We're in a gold mine, Nick. There's metal everywhere in this place. Haven't you seen the flecks of gold and other metals sparkling at us from the walls?"

"I'm a mining engineer. Of course I've seen that, and *of course* I know what it is. But this is something different. Something solid. Separate from the walls."

"I see it too." Jess stood a few yards behind them, her eyes trained up at the ledges. "From here I count three? Maybe four objects. They're long…narrow. Must be tarnished pretty badly."

Sofia squeezed her eyes shut but still could make nothing out in the distant darkness. "Wait, I know." She crouched, lowering her pack to the ground, then unholstered her camera, lifting it to her shoulder and opening out the larger fold out screen from the body. She twisted something on the lens barrel, and the display switched to a sickly green.

Nick moved behind her to take a better look as she zoomed in on the area he'd been pointing to.

"There *is* something there," Sofia said. "Four somethings—Jess you were right."

Jess moved in closer to see for herself.

"They're really narrow and…curved. But…you guys see that?" Nick placed the tip of his forefinger on the screen. "They're swaying from side to side. Like they're just…hanging there."

"They're hooks. They're fucking hooks." Jess had her hand on the camera now, pressing further on the zoom to bring more detail into the pea-coloured glow. "Nick, would there be hooks in a nineteen fifties gold mine?"

"I…uh… It's not impossible… But normally they'd be at the exit tunnel, especially if there was a vertical shaft for load lifting."

"Not like this." Jess' words were not a question.

"Not like this," Nick repeated, his voice quiet.

"What the fuck are they for then?" said Sofia, lowering the camera and flicking the switch through normal mode to standby. She holstered it and booted a large rock that was next to her, sending it ricocheting off the wall with a satisfyingly loud smack.

Nick crouched, staring down at the mine plan. "It's not marked here, but that is a hell of a high ceiling. It's possible this was an earlier entrance. That would make the lifting hooks make sense. I mean, it was that thing moving up there that drew my attention to the metal anyway."

"What did you say?" Jess stood over him, eyes wide.

"Another exit."

"Not that. You said something was moving. Up there."

Nick continued to trace the lines on the map with his forefinger. "Yeah, well, if there is another exit shaft here, it could be anything. Bats, lizards, some kind of small mammal. Who knows?"

"Did you *see* something moving up there?" Sofia had turned on her camera once more and was scouring the space above the ledge.

"I didn't see anything apart from those hooks. I heard it."

"And how far up do you suppose those ledges are, Nick?"

"According to the plans, the ceiling is a hundred and thirty-five feet up. So… Eight to ten less than that, I suppose."

"Would you hear a bat from that far away? An opossum?"

Nick rubbed his face with his hands. "It's hard to say. The acoustics of this space are pretty good and, with you both gone, the silence was pretty much absolute."

"Let's make a point of investigating any other entries up there when we get back to the surface, okay?"

Nick nodded silently as Sofia powered down the camera.

"Speaking of the surface," said Jess, retying her hair into its ponytail. "Shouldn't we be heading back out? We've been down here…almost five hours."

"You're probably right," Nick said, checking his own watch. "But I really want to finish investigating this cavern before we head back up. Fifteen minutes? What do you think?"

Jess shrugged her shoulders. "Fine with me. I'll look down the wall on the other side. Let's meet at the end, by the exit tunnels to the lowest level?"

"Deal."

They split up, Sofia staying close to Nick, taking motion shots of the textured walls, filaments of gold sparking like embers as they caught the light from the lantern. Nick stopped occasionally to inspect protrusions of rock that jutted from the wall, searching for a path to the ledges above, but none of them were grouped close enough together to get more than perhaps twenty feet off the ground.

"Jess, how are you getting on?" he called across the space, his voice reverberating around before she was able to reply.

"There are some more tools. Nothing new...more of what we found on the upper digging floor. I think some of the chisels might be a bit smaller, so I'll bag them to look at later. How about you guys?" The spotlight of her head torch wove patterns on the other side of the chamber as she spoke.

"There are some uneven patches on the wall here. I'm trying to see if there's a path up. The boots miners wore in that period were so heavy. I suppose they could have climbed with them on, but it would've been a hell of a struggle." He closed his hand around one of the protruding pieces of rock and tested his weight on it. It held firm, none of the rock cracking or crumbling. "We're almost done here. See you in a few minutes."

He continued tracing the wall, Sofia following, catching snippets of video while Nick described the features of the rock face. They reached the exit tunnel and could still see Jess on the other side of the chamber, her torch scouring high and low for tools or any evidence to help piece together the story of the mine.

Nick lowered his pack to the ground and was about to sit on it when it made a clanging sound. Sofia flicked on the camera and angled it down. He lifted the bag gingerly, revealing a curved metal rod, the arc of it folding in and then out once more, into a hook.

Crouching, Nick turned it over in his hands. One end was curled around into a crude, approximate circle. The other end looped into a point which had been filed down. It looked sharp.

Nick glanced up at Sofia. "It's too thin to lift either gold deposits or slag. It doesn't make any sense." He lifted it towards Sofia, holding it in the brighter white of her head torch beam.

"What is that, near the hoop? Is it ribbon?"

A square of fine, dark fabric had been pierced through by the hook. In the light it appeared to be a dark wine colour, though it was obscured by soil and filth. Nick tugged at the water bottle in the side pocket of his pack and splashed water onto the hook, while Sofia held the camera and torchlight utterly still on it.

Nick took the material between his fingers. "Meat," he said, and dropped the hook to the ground.

CHAPTER SIXTEEN

They sat around the table in Sofia's trailer, tumblers with several fingers of whisky in their hands. They stared at the hooked flesh, now encased in a plastic bag, like evidence in a criminal investigation.

"It's not necessarily...what it said in the note." Jess drank after she spoke, hidden behind the amber liquid in her glass.

Nick lowered his head into his hands, choosing not to respond.

"How could it have survived this long, anyway?" Jess said. "Wouldn't it have broken down? Decomposed or whatever?"

"I touched it when we brought it in, Jess. It felt like jerky." Sofia's expression was grave.

"How long can even something like that be preserved though?" Jess said. "Not Sixty odd years."

Nick thumped his fist onto the table. "I don't think the expiry date is the central issue here, Jess." He picked up the bag by the sealed top section. "And look. It *has* begun to decay. There's no telling how old this is."

"Or what meat it's made from, Nick. Calm down until we have the facts, okay?" Sofia gently pushed him to lower his arm, allowing the bag to settle back at the centre of the table. "If cannibalism is part of this story, no one is going to see your grandfather and his companions as monsters for it. They were trapped. Left to die in there. None of us know what we'd be prepared to do until we are in that situation."

Nick rubbed the thickening stubble on his chin, then drained what was left in his glass. "I'd rather talk about something else." He pulled out his copy of the mine plan, along with the two older documents he'd worked with to complete it. "I scoured these for any hint of a prior entrance above the larger chamber we were in this afternoon. There's nothing. The men must have climbed. I don't think we'll be able to get a look at what's up there. If there are more of these hooks… That or more…" The words died in his mouth.

"Are you kidding me? A hundred-foot lead climb?" Jess swallowed what was left in her glass and placed it on the counter in the kitchenette, behind her seat. "Why do you think they asked me to do this job? Haven't you seen my IGTV clip where I scaled that fractured temple wall in the jungle in Indonesia? It had, like, eighteen million views."

"Were they watching for the climb or for your short shorts?" Sofia grinned over the rim of her glass, prompting Jess to give her the finger across the table.

"Seriously though, this is my thing. And if there's something up there that's important to this story, I'll go get it."

Sofia's eyes met Nick's, and they each shrugged.

Jess continued, "I've even brought some of my climbing gear with me. I'll need a length of rope and maybe a few more gears to pin to the rock face at that height. But shit, guys, let's do this."

Sofia smiled. "Nick, we're here to tell your grandfather's story. Whatever we find up there, he's not going to be any less of a hero for saving those other miners. I've climbed before, in Peru and other places. I can't lead with my camera equipment, but I can definitely follow you, Jess, if you secure the rope."

Nick stood and walked to the trailer door, opening it and looking out into the ink-dark night. "Okay, I'll call James. See if the channel can get us the equipment."

Jess punched the air, her thrilled expression colouring her face.

"But then, I'm going to get some rest," Nick said. "Breakfast at seven?"

"Aye sir," said Sofia, playfully, with a mock salute. "Shall we get off to bed, too?" She raised her eyebrows at Jess, a grin playing on her mouth.

Nick closed the door and trudged across to his trailer.

CHAPTER SEVENTEEN

Nick stood next to the wall, two hands on the rope, angled back against the belay device on his harness. "And you're absolutely sure I'll be able to support both of your weights on this?" His words were stuttered, betraying his nerves.

"Will you stop worrying?" Jess' face was consumed by a huge grin. "I've belayed two guys of around two hundred pounds—each! And look at me! I'm tiny. I'll secure the hooks nice and tightly together, so if either of us slips, the drop is going to be no more than a few feet. You're going to be fine." She glanced over at Sofia. "Secured?"

Sofia yanked at the rope on her own harness. "Secured," she confirmed and locked off the clip on her camera holster, to keep it in place if she slipped.

"Let's go!" Jess was fast, agile, the sinewy lines of her back flexing either side of the straps of her vest as her skilled hands searched, almost on autopilot, feeling their way to secure spots and engaging her grip before her legs pushed her on and up. In no time she was six and half feet above the starter hook she'd placed, just above head height. She reached into the bag at her waist and tugged out a hook, hammering it into the rock and testing the strength of it, before attaching a quick draw and looping the rope, ready to pull it through.

"Give me some more slack, Nick!" she called down.

Nick eased some of the rope through his hands, making sure to keep the tension in the line.

"You can start ascending now, Sofia."

"Gotcha," said Sofia and scrambled up, doing her best to remember the spots where Jess' fingers had found purchase and adjusting where necessary for her shorter height.

Jess hurried on, reaching a lateral extension long enough to ease off the rope after another three stages.

"How far up am I?" she shouted down to Nick.

Nick stared up into the gloom to where the glow of Jess' head torch shone down at him. "About forty-five feet? Maybe a little more?"

"That's not much less than halfway!" Jess' smile beamed down to him, even from that distance. "I'm such a badass at this."

"Yeah, yeah, all right, miss. Those long arms and legs are a big help." Sofia was smiling up at her, one hand on the last bolt. "Shall we carry on?"

Jess flexed her fingers open and closed several times, then dug into her chalk bag to powder her fingers. "Okay, to the top now."

She scaled the next thirty feet in a matter of minutes, coordinated calls down to Nick to allow or take in more slack in the rope facilitating her rapid ascent. She drove in a bolt and heard moving rock below. She grabbed on and looked down to see Sofia dangling on the rope, turned almost ninety degrees from the wall. "Are you okay?"

Sofia's smile hadn't shifted. "I haven't done this in a couple years. I should've reacted faster to the slip. This is fun, though." She waited for the cord to spin her back to the rock face and secured herself in place. "I'm good. You can go."

Jess screamed.

Sofia's eyes widened as Jess fell from the wall and dropped a few feet, her weight jarring the entire rope. "What *was* that?" Sofia whispered.

"Something just raced across my hand." Jess held her hand, examining it for bites or some other trace of whatever it had been. It was clean, but for the white smears of climbing chalk. "It must've been a lizard, or one of those beetles we saw on day one."

Sofia shook her head. "Jess, I saw the shadow. It was *way* bigger than that."

"You're not telling me Nick's opossum theory might be right?"

Sofia grinned briefly before concern once more drew itself across her face. "I'm not convinced that's what it was."

"You guys okay up there?" Nick's bellow was quietened by the distance, the echo arriving almost ahead of the original words.

"We're fine!" Jess yelled down. "Just a small mammal trying to get friendly!" Jess climbed back on and found the bolt, searched either side of it for any sign of what had touched her hand. When there was nothing but darkness and rough rock features, she pushed on. "Twenty-five feet and we're there."

The toe of Jess' climbing shoe curled around a protruding rock feature at knee-height before she pushed off it, springing up another eight to ten feet in a matter of seconds. Her hands scrabbled around in the dark until her fingertips dug into a groove. She tensed her muscles and pushed with her legs, arriving at the very top. She reached into her bag and pulled out one final bolt, which she hammered into the wall, looping the rope through once it was secured.

She glanced down at Sofia, a dozen feet behind. "We've done it. We're here." Her breath was short. "I'm going to haul myself up and take a look around, okay?"

Sofia murmured her approval as she scaled the last few yards.

"Well?" said Sofia, shouldering the camera as she climbed to her feet.

Sofia trained the lens on Jess' face, before panning across. She seemed to almost drop the camera as she panned away from her companion to the hanging chains and ropes.

Each of them held a hook, suspended at their end. Each hook held a bounty of paper-thin, maroon material, some lined with white or yellowish fibres that ran through the fabric.

Meat.

Dried meat. Salt crystals reflected the light from Jess' head torch, like tiny gemstones, set among the flesh. "It's not... It *can't* be," Sofia said, sidestepping with the camera to capture the multitude of hooks that hung there.

"Oh no?" Jess had moved to the back of the ledge, next to the rock wall. Sofia spun to find her, then lowered the camera to her side, the red 'recording' light still flashing. Beside where Jess crouched was a rib cage, stripped bare of every scrap of flesh that had once adorned it.

"Is it...? Are you sure?" Sofia's voice wavered as she asked the question.

"Look at the size of it, Sofia. It *has* to be." She stood and covered her eyes with her hand. "Let's see what more there is up here."

They patrolled the ledge, which ran almost the length of the large cavern below, filming bones which included femurs, more ribs, and two human skulls, each lying on their sides, mouths open in an unending scream. Jess wondered whether they had been wrought onto their faces before or after their demise. More bones lay behind, heaped untidily on top of one another. Sofia raised her camera again, trembling as she took in the morbid scene.

Something moved, protruding from the pile, drawing her attention within the viewfinder. She moved closer and picked out the corner of another sheet of paper. "Jess, look." Sofia pointed with her outstretched free hand.

Jess lunged forward, carefully taking hold of the paper and lifting it out from under the scattered ivory. The paper matched that of the previous journal entries, the same curled cursive handwriting adorning the page. "Should I read—"

"No." Sofia lowered the camera and shook her head vigorously. "It has to be Nick to see it first.

"Guys!" The sound of Nick's voice stirred them from their shocked state. "Have you found anything?"

Sofia's eyes met Jess' and she shrugged, unable to find words. "We have to tell him," Jess said after a few moments. "Have to figure out what to do with all this." She moved to the edge of the outcrop of rock and looked down. "Nick... There's... We've found people up here."

Nick's hands covered his mouth, his eyes glazed over, absent. He paused for a while in silence. "So, it was true. My grandfather was... Wait, people? More than one? Are you sure? The letter only mentioned Jeffrey."

"There's another letter, Nick."

"Well...well, what does it say?"

Jess held up the paper. "It's not my place to find out. You should read it first."

Nick nodded but offered no reply.

"Nick, there's something else," Jess folded the paper, being careful to avoid damaging it, then slipped it into the side pocket of her cargo trousers. "These...remains. And the meat. We need to know what to do with it. It can't just stay up here. Can you put in a call to James?"

"Fucking hell," Nick lowered his pack to the ground and dug around for the satellite phone.

CHAPTER EIGHTEEN

May 24th.

I write this entry with trembling hands.

Two nights ago, I returned to the site of Jeffrey's burial and uncovered the body whose flesh is the only hope to sustain us. I followed the instructions of the angel, bringing a pail of water from the spring to clean off the earth and the upper layers of decay from the young American's flesh. I silently said a prayer for the bounty that our fallen comrade had provided us and another for his soul to find safe and swift passage to paradise.

From there I began to cut away at the skin with my pocketknife, paring fat and sinew as I would with a goose, were I at the Christmas table with my dear wife. I had covered the lad's face so as to shield his humanity from my sight.

Once the meat was exposed, I began to slice it, as thinly as I could. 'Like a fine ribbon' was the instruction the angel had given me. I sawed at either side of the young man's torso until the rib cage was exposed and wrapped the slices in the cleanest of the handkerchiefs I had with me in my day bag.

I took generous quantities of salt and rubbed them into the meat and then left them hanging from tarpaulin pegs which I had fashioned into crude meat hooks. These I hung in the driest space I could find, high on a ledge, where the humidity from the belly of the earth was less pronounced. All night I worked and inspected the food I was preparing for us.

When the first specks of daylight appeared through the narrow vents in the high ceiling of the large chamber, I lowered one of the hooks, testing the consistency of the meat. I felt a sickness deep within myself as my stomach growled at the touch of what was another man's muscle fibre. I can scarcely believe what six days with close to no food can do for a man's appetite. It was not quite preserved the way the angel had suggested, but the pain in my gut told me that neither I nor my fellow prisoners could wait longer if we were to survive in these harsh conditions. I lowered myself carefully from the ledge and moved as quickly as I could through the labyrinth of the mine, no longer in need of the lantern. The tunnels were etched as a map in my mind, and my eyes had adjusted somewhat to the gloomy subterranean world here.

As I returned to the dig floor we had made into our camp, Robert was just returning with two flasks of water from the spring. He asked me *where I had been, and so I decided to reveal my secret to them both, to tell them of the additional help the angel had offered.*

I opened my hand and laid the hook on the top. The meat glistened both with its own oils and with the salt crystals I had worked into it during the long night. They each tore off a piece and put them into their mouths. They described it as chewy but still quite satisfying. With a smile, I too indulged and, within moments, the meat I had brought from the new larder was spent.

Daniel asked first, where I had come upon the meat. What animal I had managed to trap in the confines of this sealed mine. None of us had seen so much as a rat after the first day of the week in which we had been stranded. I guarded a breath then revealed the truth, tempering the perhaps shocking news with the information that it was my angel—our saviour once already—who had given me the idea, and God's permission, to carry out this gruesome act so that we might live on until our eventual rescue.

Robert reacted first, covering his mouth and stumbling to his feet before retching and spitting up some portion of the meal he had just consumed. He gathered himself and looked at me with eyes I have not seen in the long years we have been workmates beneath the ground. He told me he thought me mad and said he would have no part in it. He rinsed his mouth with water from one of the flasks, spitting that onto the ground near where he had vomited up some of the meal, then disappeared from sight into one of the tunnels. I called after him to wait—that there had been no choice—but to no avail. He needed time to adjust to the idea, and that was something I was willing to accept.

Daniel was different though, silent. His eyes were closed as he still chewed the last piece of the meat he had taken from my outstretched palm. He inhaled sharply, then opened his eyes, coming closer to me. His eyes bore into mine, the sickliness that had afflicted him the last two or three days seemingly passing for an instant, replaced by madness, rage—I suppose I shall never know for certain. He spat the remaining flesh into my face, spittle and fragments of meat entering my eyes and getting caught in my filthy hair. I raised a hand to wipe it away and felt him grasp it with his and roll me to the ground.

He climbed on top of me, knees pressing sharply into my shoulders, pinning me to the hard ground. His left hand tightened at my throat, and he threw a punch with his right, connecting with my jaw. Then another to my cheek, before a rain of blows to my temple. I brought my own knees up, trying to strike the back of him without success.

Yet more blows struck me, my vision beginning to be clouded with blood and a haze that I supposed was owed to the injuries he was inflicting. I felt panic rise in my chest and, against the pain of the pressure on my shoulders I reached out with my right hand and found the water flask. I brought it up with all the force I could and struck him on the side of the head. He slipped from me and onto his side.

At this, I cannot say what possessed me—something inhuman, perhaps—but I instinctively reached into my pocket and brought out my pocketknife. I scrambled onto his prone body and plunged it into his throat once, twice. Then a third time. I fixed both hands around the blade and dragged it across, until I felt the toughness of what I imagined was the young man's windpipe.

I watched then as the light of his soul extinguished like the embers of a campfire quenched by spring rain. The boy was dead.

And I was his killer.

I covered my mouth with my free hand, only to choke as the coppery fragrance of blood was smeared around my lips.

It is *without pride or shame I confess I cried at that moment. I wept for I don't know how long.*

When the tears had dried up and I had no more to give, a light shone at the entrance to the chamber. I turned, eager to explain to Robert what had happened. But there stood the angel.

He came close to me then, clasped his cold hand to my jaw and wiped at the smear of blood that had long since dried into my skin and my scruffy beard. He told me this was all ordained by the Father. The angel revealed to me that I'd had no choice. That if only Daniel had listened to me and accepted that the action I had taken was for the good of us all, he might still be living and breathing beside me. He said Robert, too, may be dangerous in this most extreme of situations. Finally, he told me I should wrap Daniel's body in a sack and drag it to the large, cavernous place at the heart of the mine. That from this act of terrible misfortune, there would be a light.

My larder would be fuller still and, by the grace of God, I would survive.

Nicholas Jones

CHAPTER NINETEEN

Nick lay in his trailer bed, reading the letter for the eighth or ninth time that morning. James had contacted the police, who had sent in specialists to climb to the ledges, where the girls had shown them the body parts strewn across an expanse of some twenty or thirty yards. With only bone to go on, it was impossible to differentiate one body from another until they got back to the lab. The forensics team were confident they would be able to analyse the DNA and identify the individuals who had met their end down there in the mine.

Knuckles rapped gently on the door. Nick looked up from the sheaf of paper in his hand and opened his mouth, feeling how dry his tongue was, his breath violent. "It's open."

The door swung slowly open and Jess stood in the doorway, looking ready to continue the adventure. "How are you holding up?"

Nick waved the paper in the air. "How do you think?"

Jess' eyes moved down to her shoes. "We've got two days left here, Nick. We have to finish telling this story."

Nick placed the notes down on the bedside table. "Do we? Is *this* the story we came here to tell?"

Jess stepped inside and sat at the dining table opposite the bunk. "None of us knew what the story was. We only knew the very beginning. And this was not what any of us exp—"

"My grandfather was supposed to be a *hero*, Jess. He's a fucking cannibal murderer!"

Jess stood and walked towards Nick's bed. "There's a pot of coffee and breakfast in Sofia's trailer, ready and waiting for you. We *have to* finish this show. We've all signed contracts. I can't imagine how hard this is for you, but we committed to it. Whether you are with us or not, we're going back down there to finish exploring the rest of the mine and to make this show a reality. I'm not going back to this life of IGTV bullshit. This is my big shot, and I'm *going* to take it."

She strode out of the trailer and slammed the door behind her.

"Is that offer of coffee still available?" Nick stood at the open door of Sofia's trailer, his eyes on the ground.

"Of course it is. Come on in and sit down." Sofia was on her feet, moving around to the kitchenette and carving two slices of bread to drop into the toaster. "How are you feeling?"

Nick shrugged. "I don't really know, if that makes sense?"

"Confused? I think that's normal, given the situation."

Nick took a seat as Jess pushed a mug across the table towards him. He added a generous slug of creamer and took a sip, feeling his synapses sparking off the caffeine hit.

They looked at the mine plan, noting the few corners of the complex they'd not yet managed to explore.

"What more do you suppose we can expect to find?" Jess asked as she braided her long hair.

Nick sighed. "It's really tough to say. I'd expect to find more tools, the flasks they used to store water from the source. Maybe some of their clothing, if any of it survived, and it seems highly likely that there will be more notes…depending how long my grandfather lasted, of course."

Sofia set down two slices of toast in front of Nick, with jars of peanut butter, jam, and marmalade. "You forgot one thing," she said, squeezing on to the bench beside Jess. "We've only recovered two bodies. Our best guess would be that they are of Jeffrey and Daniel, the Americans. That still leaves Robert and then your grandfather."

Nick nodded as he crunched through a slice. "You're right. And, with only these two chambers at the very depths left to explore, it's difficult to say what sort of state they'll be in. It'll be seriously hot down there. Air pressure will be high and likely the humidity too."

"Could those factors affect decomposition?" Jess' eyes were wide.

"I'm not an expert, but I guess we'll find out today." Nick stuffed a triangle of toast into his mouth. "I want to thank you both for your understanding."

"Nick," Sofia reached out with her hand.

"No, I have to say this. My claustrophobia, the trauma that uncovering this terrible truth has caused…I haven't always dealt with it well, and you both…well, you've both been beyond understanding. Thank you."

Jess sat back on the bench. "Before we turn this into a support group and start doing extended group hugs, shall we get down into that mine?" She winked at Nick, who smiled back at her.

"Let's finish this thing. Two days to go, let's wrap it up." Nick quickly dashed back to his trailer to grab his day pack and head torch, and they walked back up to the entrance.

As they stood outside the gaping mouth of the mine, Jess turned around, taking in the scenery. "Among all the horror of this tale…this is such a beautiful, wild place." She pulled her phone from her pocket and snapped a few landscape photos. "To think we'll be gone in three days…" She sighed. "Okay, I'm ready."

CHAPTER TWENTY

They made swift progress through the labyrinth. Even Nick's nervous disposition towards the tight spaces was alleviated by the fact that the tunnels were now more familiar. It lacked the otherness which had magnified his mistrust of the cramped chambers and narrow walkways.

Picking up the oil lamp just before the tunnel to the cavernous space where they'd found the bodies on the ledge, they were all able to turn off their head torches to conserve batteries, the fuzzy sphere of golden light surrounding them as they proceeded to the final two tunnels at the end.

"Left or right, Mr. Engineer?" Sofia said playfully, standing between the two exit paths.

"According to the plans, they each descend at a similar angle, with an equal sized chamber underneath. I don't suppose it really matters."

Sofia shuffled over to the right. "Then I'm going to give in to one of my stupid old superstitions that I don't really believe in and choose the right-hand path, if that's okay with you guys?"

"Right it is," said Jess, and entered the enclosed space, lantern in hand.

The path began inclined at a slight angle, then dipped away quickly, each of them feeling the tension in their knees and calf muscles as they leaned back to avoid slipping. Some fifty feet or so along, it opened out into a chamber about twenty feet wide and substantially longer, the light of the lantern not quite reaching the end wall.

"Strange," said Nick as he stepped out from behind Jess and into the middle of the space. "This place was marked down as more or less square on the plans." He took a couple of steps forward into the darkness. "I still can't see the—"

Knocking sounded from above them.

Metal struck metal with a clang—once, twice.

Silence.

Jess' eyes were wide with fear as she gazed up at the ceiling.

"Nick, take a look at this." Sofia was crouched, her camera tuned onto another shred of paper.

Nick paced over, the sound of him swallowing audible against the background of silence.

May 29th, 1957

Am I even a man anymore after what I have done? I look at my hands and see not the tools that have served me so well in my lifetime, but weapons. Poor Robert.

Nicholas Jones

For the second time in less than a day, Nick's hands trembled as his eyes scanned back and forth over a written discovery. "What happened to Robert?" he asked aloud, without any real intention to do so.

"I suppose we can guess, after yesterday," said Jess, coming closer to read through the note for herself. "Let's see if there's more down here."

She stepped forward into the thick, inky darkness that occupied the rear of the chamber, the light from the lantern spreading out onto the walls, casting long, dancing shadows behind the three of them, while Nick stowed the note in his bag.

Thirty feet into the room, she paused. "Still no sign of the far wall. Weird!"

"Keep going," Sofia said, her voice hushed.

Another series of bangs behind them. Faster this time, more percussive. Violent, even.

They stopped still.

"What the fuck *is* that?" Sofia said, spinning with the camera to her eye.

"Probably an animal," Nick said under his breath. "I hope they don't make too much mess."

"I hope they don't come down here after us." Sofia turned back to face front.

"Come on," said Jess, and continued on.

"Stop," shouted Sofia, after a few more steps.

"What is it?" Jess' voice was higher pitched than usual. Strained.

"Over there," said Sofia. "I caught it in my night vision."

Jess swung the lantern in the direction Sofia's outstretched finger pointed, illuminating a heap of something. Some kind of heavy fabric. They rushed over to it and bent down.

"Mining overalls," said Nick, picking at the pile. "Oh, fuck me," he said, and dropped it, wiping his hands on his trousers. The fabric was stained a deep brown.

Blood.

Enough to imply that someone had not walked away from this scene.

"They must have been Robert's. He must be…" Jess let the words die in her mouth.

"We'll collect these up later. Come back with a bag," said Nick. "Let's find the back of this chamber."

A low, sustained rumble sounded behind them.

"*Animals?*" said Jess, incredulous. "We should go and take a look. At least one of us. What if someone is tampering with the entrance again?"

"Relax. The ground isn't moving. It can't be the entrance caving in," said Nick, taking the lantern and stepping further into the chamber.

"Thanks, that makes me feel *so* much better," said Jess, staying close to him and Sofia.

"Here," said Nick, and crouched to his knees once more.

June 4th, 1957

Robert was watching me today. I saw him, though I'm not certain he realised. He can't climb like I can. Cannot see in the dark like I can. Hasn't adjusted to this place in the way I have. He should have listened to me. To the angel. He was watching me as I prepared the meat from the Americans. Perhaps he has seen the error of his judgement. Perhaps he will join me. Perhaps he will not and he wishes ill upon me.

Time will tell.

Nicholas Jones

"Is anyone else finding these notes crazier and crazier?" Jess took the paper from Nick's hand. "Even the writing is more eccentric. Compare this to the earlier ones...the letters are wild, angular. What was happening to him?"

Nick snatched the paper bag. "He was going fucking insane." He shook his head and stuffed the letter into his pack. "He was trapped down here, hallucinating this *angel* of his. And then the desperation...what it made him do..."

"Guys," Sofia stepped between the two of them. "Let's find Robert's remains and get out of here. I don't like those sounds from up there one bit. We can talk about all of this later."

Jess and Nick were quiet but pressed on into the unfolding dark. Finally, up ahead, a wall ghosted out of the gloom, framed with wooden beams.

"He's not here," Nick said, as much to himself as anything else.

"Robert or your grandfather?" Jess' voice had a spikiness to it.

"Neither of them. They're both down here somewhere, but not here." Nick thought back to the letter, his grandfather's words, 'poor Robert.' If he had killed him, as they all expected was the case, why would he allow himself to die in the same space Robert's remains occupied. "We should get to the final chamber this morning. Get this done with."

The bassy rumbling sound began again, sustained for longer this time. Nick lurched towards the exit, the lantern swinging and casting shadows which melded, merged, and contorted across the uneven walls of the chamber.

"Wait, Nick," Sofia's voice held him back. He turned to face her, her features obscured by the blackness. "Another paper. There, in the corner. I noticed it when you took off."

Nick took measured steps into the corner and lowered himself to a crouch.

June ??, 1957

The angel walks these tunnels no more. I am alone. Alone but for guilt and hunger. And from that self-same hunger, yet more guilt. What am I becoming?

Nicholas Jones?

"What does it say?" Sofia said.

Nick held his crouched position, unflinching.

"Nick, the letter?" Jess stood over him.

"Read it for yourself, I'm going to the final chamber." He thrust the note into her hand and dashed from the room, up into the steep, sloping tunnel then back out into the huge cavern.

Stones skittered and crunched yards away from him. Nick froze. He looked into the swaying light as the lantern swivelled back and forth in his hand, the handle groaning against the silence.

"Who's there?" Nick shouted.

He thought he heard breathing ahead of him. He set the lantern on the ground and reached up to the grip of his head torch. He squeezed it and twisted, a flood of dazzling white opening in front of him. There was nothing there.

Empty space.

"Nick!" Sofia's voice was harsh as she exited the tunnel. "What the fuck? You should have waited for us!"

Nick turned to them, feeling his cheeks redden in embarrassment at having fled. "I'm sorry. This is just becoming more nightmarish with every passing—"

"Oh, my God." Jess pointed at something beyond Nick's shoulder.

He spun as quickly as he could, his head torch illuminating a fragment of a shadow as it disappeared into one of the tunnels at the end of the cavern.

"What the *fuck* was that?" Jess retreated to the wall and lowered herself almost to the ground.

"It was fast," Nick said. "Could be a wolf, I guess, or some other canine. I heard it breathing, you know? Just before you guys got up here."

"It was *that* close?" Sofia's voice wavered. "That's it, I say we get out now. We can come back for the last chamber tomorrow. See if James or Al can get us some kind of protection."

"We can't stop now. This is the last place. The only chamber left unexplored. And besides, if we rush out there now, we're more likely to spook it and then ... well, who knows?" Nick twisted off his head torch and scooped up the lantern. "There are going to be more remains down here, and this time, one set is going to be my grandfather's."

"Are you sure you're ready to see that?" Jess' anger seemed to have flowed out of her with the fleeing animal.

"What did you say in the trailer this morning? We signed contracts to tell this story. We *have* to finish it. I'm ready."

CHAPTER TWENTY-ONE

The tunnel into the final chamber was the tightest they had encountered. They crept in single file, scarcely any light from the lantern making it past the body of Jess at the front, Nick and Sofia in near-total darkness. Nick's breath was ragged, a sheen of sweat coated his face and forearms. As with the entrance on the other side, the path was on a gentle slant at first and then dove into the bowels of the mine, rocks slipping underfoot as they moved.

After fifteen yards or so, the room widened, the light ghosting outward, illuminating everything. The space was tiny in comparison to the one they had been in moments earlier. At the centre of the room was a brown cloth bag. The material looked like it had been treated with a chemical or a varnish to protect it from decay. Besides that, the chamber was empty.

"It's too small," Nick said, approaching it. He touched the material with his fingertips and, finding it dry, gripped the fabric. "Where are the remains?" He glanced around to Jess and Sofia. "Should I pick it up?"

Jess closed her eyes and inhaled deeply.

"We have to know what's in there," Sofia said and squeezed Jess' hand in her own.

Nick closed his hand around the material and lifted the bag up. Underneath, on the ground, was a human skull. The lower jaw was cleaved in two, but had been put back into place, slightly ajar. Inside the mouth had been stuffed another sheet of old paper. Nick grasped it and tried to pull it out. The teeth resisted, requiring him to prise the jaw open, his fingers digging uncomfortably into the nasal cavities to find grip. He slid out the paper and removed his hand from the bone. His breath short, he unfolded it.

June, 1957

Robert came to me today, while I was resting on the lowest levels of the mine. Sleep is something long departed, yet still I require rest after endless days carving and preparing meat or toiling with picks and shovels near the collapsed exit tunnels in the hope of finding our escape.

I lay on my back on a torn sack, my eyes closed, when Robert moved into the chamber without saying a word. I heard him before he was close enough to present any danger and opened my eyes wide, fixed them on him, to show him that any attempt on me by surprise was foolishness.

He spoke my name and, in that moment, I felt a spark of kindness, of the kinship we have fostered over the many years as friends— nay, brothers—below the surface. I greeted him and offered him my hand, but he shook his head, holding his place against the ragged wall.

He began to tell me that he was afraid. Both of what I was doing and of what I had become. A madness, a sickness, he told me, had overcome me, and now I was acting not from my own mind but from the disease that had gripped me in its clutches.

I told him that everything I did was because of the angel. Because of his words, his pardon from our Lord for my deeds, as they were necessary under the circumstances.

Robert stopped me then, blindsided me, asked me why it was I had been shown the grace of God and not he or the American boys, Daniel and Jeffrey, God rest them. For that I had no answer. I was quiet, thoughtful.

Then a light filled the room, and the answer was there with us. The angel appeared, and through his light and grace, I would be reconciled. I spoke to him directly, asking him why I had been chosen and for him to tell my dear friend Robert.

Robert became pale, his eyes like saucers. He asked me who I was talking to. I gestured to the angel, tried to explain, but Robert moved closer, placed his hands on my shoulders. At first, I thought his intention was to comfort me, but the angel showed me his true desire, drawing my eye to the short-handled pick in Robert's belt.

I thrust my right shoulder into him, setting him off balance, and reached for the pick. Grasping the handle, I thrust it upward, striking him across the chin. My heart stopped as I witnessed the damage the blade had done, his jaw coming apart and blood...so much blood.

Still he was alive. He swiped at me, knocking the pick from my hand. I bolted from the chamber and up the path to the cavern. Robert was close behind, in spite of his injury. I arrived at the wall and began to scale it, aiming for the ledge, and a height I supposed he could not reach.

I was convinced I was at the top and reached out, but Robert was closer than I realised, pulling at my trailing leg. I grasped at one of the hooks, and it trembled under my weight, some of the rock above coming loose. The rocks fell. I ducked my head, but Robert was unsighted. I turned in time to see the wire the hook had been suspended by slice into his neck. His head peeled back unnaturally. I reached out with my free hand, but it was too far.

He crashed to the ground, his head coming clean off in the impact. Robert was gone, in the most awful fashion.

The angel stood beside him, eyes fixed on mine.

I told him that Robert would not meet the fate of the other men.

I wept for a long time, before digging a pit in which to incinerate his body.

Nicholas Jones

Nick passed the letter to Sofia. She and Jess were silent as they read.

Nick's eyes were drawn to the back of the chamber, off to the left. Something gaped in the darkness. With Sofia and Jess distracted, he moved forward and crouched down, twisting the beam on his head torch to its brightest setting. The rounded, elongated hole was barely half full, flecks of grey cinders in a series of piles.

"Guys," he called out. "Here."

They joined him, staring into the torchlight.

"This is all that's left? It looks so small…insignificant," said Jess, rising to her feet, pulling her arms into her body.

Nick stood to join her. "Well, if you think about it, when you bring your family member home from a funeral, the ashes are normally contained in those urns, which are so sma—"

A huge, distant boom stole Nick's words.

"What the hell *was* that?" Sofia moved to the entrance of the chamber, the cone of light from her head torch trailing up the tunnel. "I'm going to see what's going on up there. I'll be quick. And careful." She hurried into the tunnel and out of sight.

"Sofia, wait!" Jess was standing at the exit to the tunnel, peering upward into the gloom. She turned back. "Nick, are we just going to let her go up there alone? We don't know what kind of animals might be up there."

Nick picked up the oil lantern, still burning, from the corner. "Those noises are not from animals."

"How do you know that?"

"They're from something far worse."

"What do you mean by that?"

"People, Jess. It's the only explanation for the sounds we've been hearing. Let's find Sofia before she gets into trouble."

CHAPTER TWENTY-TWO

"Sofia," Jess shouted as loudly as she could into the cavern above. "Hey!"

The sound bounced around the tunnel, echoes striking at them from out of the darkness. They held still, listening for some sound of Sofia's footfalls. The rushing and rumbling of the spring pool, only a few hundred yards away, provided the sonic backdrop. No other sounds could be heard.

"Where is she, Nick?" Worry and fear contorted Jess' face.

Nick knitted his hands in front of his mouth and thought. "If she was looking for the source of the sounds, there's no way it could be in here, or in the bowels of the mine, where we were. It's either the tools on the digging floor above, or..."

"Or...?"

"Or the exit. The supports. Come on!"

They covered the length of the gaping cavern in impossibly short time, reaching the ramp-like tunnel to the digging chamber above in a matter of moments. The incline slowed their progress, Nick especially. Jess stopped near to the exit and reached out, taking Nick's hand and hauling him up the last few yards.

The room was dark. Quiet. Empty but for the rack of tools they'd found there during the first few days.

Jess sprinted to the upward tunnel, turning back to where Nick was fiddling with the tools. "Nick, come on!"

Nick grasped a pickaxe and a shovel and carried them over to Jess, handing her the pick. "We might need these."

Jess nodded.

They turned and strode up towards the entrance floor. The space was in total darkness but for a small light source some thirty yards away.

Nick looked at his watch. "No, no, no, no, NO!"

"What the hell is it?"

"It's not even seven, Jess. It's still half daylight."

"But...oh, *fuck!*"

"Exactly."

"But Al's team. The supports. They were doubled up. There were no earthquakes. How could it all have collapsed?"

Nick put his hand on Jess' shoulder. "Someone did this. This was *not* an accident."

Jess took a step backward. "I've just realised..." She darted ahead into the darkness, leaving the pick to fall to the ground with a thwack. She crouched down next to the light and lifted Sofia's camera to her shoulder. The side screen was flipped open and the camera was still on the night vision setting, illuminating the room in sickly green.

Nick came closer. "Sofia's?"

Jess nodded.

"Did she record anything on there before—"

Jess hushed him before he could get the words out and puzzled at the buttons on the barrel and main body of the camera. She slid a switch into 'playback' mode and was presented with a grid of thumbnails, the last one showing up as only four minutes old. She glanced up at Nick, then pressed play.

The screen showed darkness, only the strip of light from Sofia's head torch illuminating anything. The display suddenly lit up in the green of night vision. The recording was silent until Sofia began to speak. "This is the place the sound seemed to be coming from. Some fucker has sabotaged the support struts. We're stuck down here again."

The camera panned along the floor of the mine entrance, the hydraulic devices lying on their sides, some pierced, dark fluid seeping from them like blood from wounds.

The sound of moving rocks was picked up by the camera, which began to tremble. "Hello? Who's there. Fucking hell."

The camera's eye darted upward revealing something clinging to the ceiling. Arms, legs, rippled with lithe muscle tissue, clinging to the rocks above. The back, too, was sinewy, yet emaciated, lines of taut strength somehow married to visible bones, just below the surface. The camera moved backward, looking up at a tighter angle.

"Oh, my God," Sofia said, her voice trembling. "*Dios me salve!*"

The neck arched backwards, revealing a face topped with thin, lank hair, hanging down almost into the lens. The mouth opened, revealing spaces where the majority of the front teeth had once been. The eyes were deep set, dark, wild. The thing dropped from the ceiling, Sofia screamed, and the camera fell to the ground. The recording fizzled to nothing and then cut out altogether.

CHAPTER TWENTY-THREE

"What the hell was that?" Jess sat on her pack, her knees pulled in tight to her body, tears streaming down her cheeks.

Nick held the camera, watching those final moments where the creature leaned back, exposing its face, over and over. "It's not possible." He shook his head from side to side, then tracked back in the recording to watch it again, rolling the camera to an upside-down position. "But it is. Oh my fucking God, it is."

"Is what?" Jess wiped a trail of snot from her nose on to a tissue she'd pulled from her pack.

"Not what, Jess. *Who*." Nick closed the side screen and placed the camera on the ground, lowering his pack and sitting on it. "He's wiry, his joints are swollen and his movements are overly cumbersome—probably to do with the lack of sunlight. But that was him. I can still see the man he once was in those mangled features."

"Nick, what are you talking about?"

"That was my grandfather."

Jess grabbed the camera and flipped open the screen, finding the spot and freeze-framing the image. "This *thing* doesn't even look human. Look at it, the way the muscles are so defined in some places and then the skin just barely covering bone in others. It's not a man. Much less a man in his eighties."

Nick reached into his pack and found the sheaf of journal entries from his grandfather. Finding the one they had recovered at the very base of the mine, he read from the page. "'Am I even a man anymore after what I have done?' Those were his words Jess. And you said it yourself, his handwriting had changed from beautiful cursive script to the slashes and angular strokes of a madman."

"But Nick, look at that face." The paused video somehow made the already monstrous visage into something even more vile. Muscles in motion, captured at an angle that rendered them as far from human as any face either of them had ever seen. "Look at the eyes. The way they are so far back in the skull. It's *hideous*."

Nick nodded. "You're right about all of that. But I know the lines of that face. Looked at it so many times on my grandmother's dresser when I was a kid. Hell, I even have that picture of him from the local paper, when the news of his and Robert's demise was first made public. I've no doubt. It's him."

"Was. It *was* him. Whoever he was, this thing is not him. Not really."

She closed the camera and placed in into her pack, between some items of clothing for padding. "What do we do now? Where has he taken Sofia?"

Nick dug into his bag, retrieving the satellite phone. "First, we call James and tell him about the sabotage. If nothing else, we need this mine opened. Then, we start searching. There's nothing else we can do."

"Okay. That sounds like a plan. How much food do we have?" Jess dug into her pack, pulling out some energy bars, and some dehydrated fruit.

"Not much," said Nick trawling through his own pack and coming up with a similar stash. "Sofia had the meal packs. Let's hope they can get us out quickly. But first, let's find her." He stood and took stock of the devastation that had been caused to the support struts once more. "It must've taken incredible strength to buckle these. Remember what Al said last time?"

Jess murmured her agreement.

"Maybe he is…something else."

"That wasn't a man in that clip, Nick. That wasn't your grandfather."

Nick wrapped his arms around Jess, kissed her on top of the head. "We're going to find her. It's going to be okay."

Jess looked up at him and forced a smile onto her face, though her eyes betrayed the lie. "First we call James. Then we go find her. Let's go."

CHAPTER TWENTY-FOUR

Nick disconnected the call and stuffed the sat phone back into his pack. "He's going to put in a call to Al now. I tried to estimate how far back the entrance has collapsed, but they're going to need to use some ground radar and some other tools before they can start to dig us out again. It's deeper than the last time."

"How long is that gonna take?" Jess tousled her hair loose from its braid.

"James said they'll try to make it hours rather than days."

"They'll *try*? Jesus."

"They can only do what they can do, Jess. He knows Sofia is missing, so…" He trailed off. "But look, we're wasting time. Let's start searching."

Jess picked up the lantern, a grim expression wrought across her face and set out in front of Nick, towards the tunnels to the lower sections of the mine. At the tunnel entrance, she paused. "You know, we haven't been through this tunnel." She gestured towards the mine cart tunnel, its slim rails still gleaming in places, badly tarnished in others.

"It's awfully steep, Jess. I'm not sure I can without ropes."

"I'm not asking you to. But I think I can manage. He... It could be hiding her anywhere."

Nick peered into the tunnel, noticing how much steeper it was than the foot tunnel. "This leads straight down, two levels below, doesn't it?"

"Exactly. That's an awful lot of space we haven't surveyed."

"How are you going to support yourself? Prevent yourself from sliding and hurting yourself?"

Jess moved closer, peered in, holding the lantern in front of them. "I'll leave the lantern with you, use the rail sleepers as supports for my feet, and use my climbing gloves, so I can lean into the walls."

Nick sighed. "I don't know if this is a good idea. But then, we saw how he could climb. This is exactly the kind of place he could exploit, knowing we couldn't get in there."

Jess handed the lantern to Nick and boosted herself up and into the tunnel, having to crouch to squeeze into the smaller, cart-sized space.

"Wait," said Nick. "Stay there until I can get down to the bottom. At least I can give you some support if you start to slide."

Jess nodded. "Good idea. But hurry, this is seriously uncomfortable."

Nick took off, hurtling down the first tunnel and into the wide unloading area. Barely stopping to look around, he hurried to the passage at the end. He surveyed the narrow space and shivered. He closed his eyes, took a breath, and dove in, his feet scuffing on the uneven ground as he strode down to the digging face room. He hesitated, listening for any sound from Sofia or her captor. The space was silent but for his own heavy breaths.

He turned to the cart tunnel and leaned in. "Jess," he called out, his arm resting on the bottom sleeper of the railway track. "I'm in position." Echoes bounced up the cramped walls.

"Okay!" She yelled back. "I'm coming down!"

The sound of feet skidding and rocks tumbling echoed down the tunnel, magnified and metamorphosed by its tubular shape. Nick stepped back to avoid any falling debris.

Above, Jess planted her feet between the advancing sleepers, trying to slow herself as the incline seemed to increase and her rugged descent began to resemble falling. "Fuck, fuck, fuck!" she shouted as she hugged the wall on her right with her shoulder, the uneven surface grazing her skin.

She scanned the underside of the tunnel as she moved, trying to approximate how far she had gone, how far she had left to go. She reached out with her right arm. It slid into a crevice, and she stopped. Sharp pain shot up her arm, the tension in her elbow joint causing her to cry out.

"Jess! Are you okay?" Nick's voice was far closer than it had been, giving her at least some sense of relief.

She bit her lip. "I'm fine. Just jarred my arm. But I think I've found something. She stepped into the crack in the earth and found an almost-flat surface carved into the rock face. Upon it was another smaller lantern which was unlit and beside it, three photographs, fanned out on the surface. Faces looked up at her from another time and place.

The first was of two people. One was the man she recognised, both from Nick's news cutting and now from the terrifying face on the video. The other was a smiling woman beside him, young and vibrant, with rolling curls on her head and a smile that seemed to glow from the image. The next was of an infant, the name 'Anthony' and a date in 1955 scrawled below him. Finally, there was another of Nicholas, this time with his arm around another man. The scene was so familiar. The outside of the mine had barely changed in all these sixty years.

Jess scooped up the images and stuffed them into the side pocket of her trousers. She thought about taking the lamp, too, but had second thoughts about fragments of broken glass flying in all directions as she sped down the tunnel. She was about to move back out to restart her descent when she noticed something else—a silver cross on a chain, badly tarnished. The lower portion of the cross had been bent, twisted, and looped around. She pulled out the photos once again. In each of the two he was featured in, Nicholas was wearing the same cross around his neck.

But no more.

She stashed it with the photos and slid down the remainder of the tunnel.

CHAPTER TWENTY-FIVE

Nick stared at the photos, then at the cross in his hand, the bend had almost ruptured the metal. "He was wearing this in the photo from the newspaper cutting, too." He stuffed the cross and chain into the side pocket of his pack. "I wonder why he took it off. And why he defaced it this way."

"Remember the last note we found. The *angel* had abandoned him. Maybe he was bitter. About their predicament."

Nick nodded and carefully placed the photos in the document holder with the journal pages. "We need to find Sofia, fast. If we delay too long…well, we know what happens to people down here, since the original cave-in."

"Let's get to the cavern. It's where he stored the other bodies."

Jess began across the chamber without waiting for a reply, her fists clenching and unclenching. They entered the narrow downward tunnel in single file, the air silent except for the skittering of dislodged stones and the grips of their shoes biting into the surface. After a few minutes of walking, they came out into the open space of the cavern, the light from the lantern in Nick's hand melting into the abundant darkness.

"Shall we check the high ledges?" Nick started forward, towards the far wall.

"Wait," Jess yanked him back. "Let's be sensible. First, we go to the spring, fill our water flasks. We won't be able to do this if we faint from dehydration. We don't feel it because of the humidity down here, but we *have* to be prepared." She crouched and fished her flask from the side pocket of her pack, then reached out a hand. "Give me yours. I'll run, then bring them both back. You stay here with the weapons. If anything moves, shout as loud as you can."

Nick glanced around, found nothing but dark, empty space. Icy fingers traced their way up his spine. After all his problems with claustrophobia, he could do nothing but smile as he realised it was here, in a chamber the size of a football field, the roof a hundred and thirty feet above him, that his fear had reached its breaking point. "I know you're right. It's the quickest way. But please...hurry. We should try to avoid being alone."

Jess sprang to her feet, lowering the angle of her head torch to better see the terrain in front of her. She took Nick's hand in both of hers and squeezed. "Two minutes," she said, and disappeared, a meandering shaft of light and the diminishing crunch of her boots the only trace left of her.

Nick watched until the light disappeared into the tunnel at the far corner of the cavern, then turned to watch the wide-open space in front of him, detecting movement in the shadows that could just as well have been an invention of his terrified mind. "Hello," he said, his voice quiet, hoping not to receive a response.

A wall of silence came back to him, magnifying the sound of the blood pumping in his eardrums.

Then he caught something. Shuffling. The movement of dislodged rock and then a murmur of voice. Muffled. But unmistakably Sofia's.

Panic chipped away at the fear that gripped him. He stepped forward, into the dark, the fuzzy bubble of light from the lantern moving with him. "Sofia!" He shouted her name into the darkness, feeling the pull in his vocal cords.

No response.

Again, he called out. This time a distorted groan travelled back in response.

He turned to the direction of the spring. "Jess, Sofia's close! Hurry!"

As he waited for her reply, a different sound rolled across the space towards him. Like the low rumble of distant thunder. A bass frequency, gravelly, part animal, yet somehow bearing a human quality. Nick felt his breathing gather pace. He stepped backward, his foot almost slipping on loose stones. He righted himself and swallowed, the gulping sound filling the space around him.

"Sofia," he shouted again, despite the metallic taste of fear and the dryness in his mouth. "Are you okay?" The sound of his voice echoed around the cavern.

The growl returned, louder this time, more present. A rumble, sustained and with a visceral rasp to it. Fighting the urge to run, he took a step forward, held the light high in front of his face.

Something reached out from behind, grasping Nick's shoulder. He let out a cry of surprise, spinning, and brought up his hands to block out the blinding white light of Jess' head torch. "Fuck, Jess! You almost scared me to death!"

She grinned, waving two flasks in front of him, the liquid gurgling inside. "What the hell was that noise?" She said, suddenly looking more serious.

Nick flicked his head over his left shoulder. "It was him. It. They're up there, I'm sure of it."

"Sofia too?" Jess' eyes widened.

"I heard her. I couldn't make out any words. She could be gagged or hurt. But I heard her voice, no doubt."

Jess nodded. "Let's get to the wall."

They stuffed the flasks into their packs and raced towards the far wall with the ledges. "No! No, no, no!" Jess darted ahead, stopping just before she slammed into the rock surface.

Nick jogged to catch up to her. "What is it? What's the matter?"

"Look at the rock face." She gesticulated wildly towards the high ledges. "He's taken the rope."

Nick covered his face with his hands, then pulled them away. "We're going to have to wait 'til they can get into the cave, fetch more rope...or build a scaffold."

Jess tugged at her hair. "Do you think she'll survive that long? You said it yourself, we *know* what happens to people down here." She gazed up at the rock face, a determined look fixed on her face. "Fuck it, I'll have to free climb it."

CHAPTER TWENTY-SIX

"Jess, wait," Nick tugged at her arm. Jess reluctantly turned to face him. "Do you really think this is a good idea? Look up there. It's over a hundred feet. If you slip—"

"It's game over. I *know*." Jess' face flushed red with heat. "But we can't leave her up there with that thing. *I* can't leave her. Better to die trying than to sit here and listen to him… I don't even want to think about it." She glanced up at the rock face. "I think I remember where most of the good holds are."

Nick wrung his hands and nodded. "Okay. You're right. What can I do?"

Jess tugged her hair loose, before retying it in a tighter ponytail and fixing her head torch in place, twisting it fully on for maximum illumination. "Well, when I reach the top, I'll tie off the rope up there and then throw you the slack. I'll need to abseil down, possibly carrying Sofia, depending on her condition."

"And what about while you ascend?" Nick's voice stuck in his dry throat.

"Cross your fingers. And move the fuck out of the way if I fall." Jess winked at him and reached into her pack, pulling out the chalk bag. She affixed it to the belt on her shorts and then dipped her right hand in before pulling it out and smoothing the white powder over her palms and fingertips on both hands. "It's going to be fine," she said, glancing up again. "See you in half an hour or so."

Nick stepped back as she sprang forward and grasped at the rock. Her fingers probed for secure holds then her legs lifted her upward. The cavern was silent now, the distant moaning of Sofia quieted, the growls of Nick's grandfather gone for now. Nick angled the lantern upward, Jess growing ever more distant as her feet scrabbled at the rough rock face.

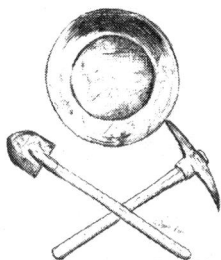

Ten minutes in and the muscles in her forearms were screaming. She lifted her right leg onto a protrusion of rock and pulled herself tight to the wall, with her left arm locked in position. She pulled her right arm away from the wall and flexed it, feeling the lactic acid build-up discharging.

"Are you okay?" Nick's voice from below sounded distant, as though from another place altogether.

"I'm fine. It's just tough with no chance to rest. I'll be okay." She switched hands and flexed the left, opening the joints in her fingers.

Then her hands were back on the rockface, securing her position. She pushed upward and onward, beyond halfway, the ledges now in sight.

She stretched, clinging to the first section of the overhang. She breathed in and pulled with all her strength, lifting her left leg until she found a nook, then pushed her body up. She hung there, conscious of being at almost forty-five degrees to both the wall and the ground, which was now some sixty yards below. She took another breath and powered on to the next place with decent grip. Her left leg stretched outward, almost at full extension, finding a jut that allowed her a moment of relative ease for her hands. Then the sound reached her. Sofia's voice, starting at a whimper and rising to a wail.

"Sofia!" Jess called out, her chest heaving, the sting in her fingers suddenly amplified.

No reply came.

Jess bit down on her lip, whispering to herself that she had to go on. She glanced down at Nick who stood wringing his hands below. "Did you hear that?" Her voice echoed around the chamber.

Nick closed his eyes, nodded.

The howling came again, quieter this time. Jess burst forward, her feet skittering on sharp edges as she hauled her tired body upward, her eyes blinking away tears. "Wait, Sofia. Wait, wait, wait. I'm coming," she spoke the words softly to herself. But they gave her strength, resolve. She exhaled, groaning as she heaved herself over the final point of the overhang and boosted herself up with her legs, back onto the vertical. Ten yards from the ledge.

She engaged her arms one at a time, taking the chance to flex her arms and fingers again. Placing both hands back on to the rockface, she looked upward, mentally planning the final push. "Here we fucking go."

Like a spider, her limbs folded and unfolded, seemingly independent of one another as they traced the jagged wall. She sought out one grip point, then engaged and probed for the next. She made up the first seven or eight yards in moments before her eyes darted up to the ledge to find the best path to the top. They froze on two amber circles in the darkness.

Eyes.

The irises stretched, as if belonging to a cat about to strike, then the thing moved forward, crawling down the rockface towards her, inverted. The emaciated, yet somehow-sinewy body sickened her as it crawled closer, fingers bereft of nails pinching at the rock, securing it in place. Thin, wiry hair hung lank over its face as it eyed her, neck cracking as it strained, eyes just a few short yards from her own.

The thing opened its mouth, trying to shape its blistered, dry lips, revealing a jaw that bore scant few teeth other than the upper and lower incisors. Behind them was the stub of a long-removed tongue. Its breath came: hot, dry, and foul. It moved its mouth more now. As if trying to speak.

Jess felt her hands trembling. Her grip had been clasped at the same spot for too long. "Let. Sofia. *Go*," she spat.

The thing's eyes narrowed. Its mouth clamped shut and nostrils flared. Then it lashed out, bursting forward and striking a blow at Jess' left shoulder.

Jess squeezed with all the strength in her right hand, as her left flailed. Her body twisted and she watched, as though outside herself, as she lost her grip and tumbled head-first. She lifted her head, narrowly avoiding a sharp outcrop then flung out both hands. She grasped the point of the overhang and held on, engaging her biceps and pulling herself tight to the wall. She kicked out with her legs, finding nothing, her right knee slamming into hard stone. She yelped out loud with pain. Her fingers began to slip. Her right hand came loose. She began to fall back.

It's over, she thought.

She closed her eyes and threw her right hand with everything she had left and found an edge. Squeezing, she kicked out with her left leg, and found something. Pushing upward, she hung there, waiting for the pendular motion to halt. Then she was still, aside from her heaving lungs.

Jess glanced down at her right knee. Warm blood trickled from the gash that had opened over the kneecap. Then movement from above snapped her attention back to her attacker. Once again, she saw the eyes first as it crawled towards her, its naked body close to the rock face, lizard-like in the way it traversed the wall. Its mouth opened again, the gelatinous black base of the tongue fidgeted in the space between its two pairs of opposing canines. It shifted back, as if readying itself to pounce.

"Close your eyes! Now!" Nick's voice echoing off the rock walls.

Jess scrunched her eyes closed and squeezed her jaw shut, waiting for the blow that would send her down to oblivion. She heard a ripping sound from below and then a blinding flash that burned at her retinas, even with them hidden behind her closed eyelids.

A scream rang out through the cavern, high-pitched and visceral. Then darkness returned. Jess opened her eyes.

It was gone.

CHAPTER TWENTY-SEVEN

"What the fuck *was* that?" Jess screamed as she lay on her back on the ledge, her chest heaving with difficult, rapid breaths.

"A flare. I just figured…if he was used to the dark…"

"You saved my fucking life." Her words were likely too quiet to travel the distance to Nick, on the cavern floor.

Jess lifted her head from the stone and looked down at her knee. Blood seeped from the gash. Reaching into her backpack she pulled out a spare vest top, holding it in both hands and tearing it down the middle. She took one half of the fabric and wrapped it tightly around the joint, blood immediately discolouring the pale material.

Sofia's voice drifted across the ledge, more a croak than a cry now. The sound injected energy into Jess' tired limbs, urging her to roll on to her side and push up to a crouch. She glanced both ways, looking for any sign of Nick's grandfather, then dashed towards the source of the sound.

Nick watched her creep along the visible area of the ledge until she was enveloped by shadow. All he could do now was wait. He cursed himself for his powerlessness. Stuck down there on the chamber floor, he was powerless to intervene. Powerless to protect his companions. And alone, should the creature find its way down to ground level.

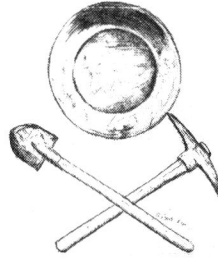

Jess lowered herself to a crouch as the shadowy cave wall covered her, aiming her head torch down at the craggy ground. She carefully placed her feet between the rocks as she entered the natural enclosure where they had found the remains, days earlier.

Pressing herself to the wall, peering into the almost liquid darkness, she heard movement. Scratching. Shuffling. "Sofia!" she whispered.

More shuffling.

She sidestepped around the natural doorway and into the gloomy chamber. At the distant edge of her torchlight, a human shape was stretched out, unnaturally, arms suspended above head height, torso elongated. Jess burst forward. She placed her hands on Sofia's face.

Sofia's eyelids fluttered, but she remained unconscious. A swollen lump above her left eye stood as testament to the knockout blow struck by the thing.

She reached up to where Sofia's hands were fastened together with the climbing rope and untied them. They fell to her sides lifelessly, Jess just managing to reach in and take her weight before lowering her to the ground. Sofia flailed like a rag doll. Jess rolled her onto her back and pressed her fingers to her neck, finding a slow but persistent pulse. She pulled back one of her eyelids, finding a heavily dilated pupil Probably concussed. The superficial cuts to Sofia's neck and arms were in no way life threatening.

Jess felt a tear tumble down her cheek and fall onto Sofia's midriff. She wiped her eyes and stood, unhooking the climbing rope from where it had been hung. After coiling the rope around her shoulder, she crouched and hooked Sofia's arm around her neck before easing her up into a fireman's carry. She pushed gently up with her legs, swaying under the weight as she stabilised herself, then began to move towards the exit of the monster's food store.

"Nick," she cried out as she exited the enclosed space and moved out onto the ledge. She surged forward, out of the shadow.

"You found her? Thank God," Nick's voice wavered as he called back to her.

"Listen, I'm going to fix the rope, then tie her into a harness, and you're going to have to ease her to the bottom. Can you do that for me?"

Nick rubbed his hand over his face, then nodded. "I can. You'll have to guide me, but yes. Yes, I can."

Jess grimaced under the dead weight. She took the final few steps to the ledge and lowered Sofia's body gingerly to the ground. Then she was on her feet and reaching into her pack for a hook. She moved close to the ledge and dug the gear into the rock floor, twisting it so that the thread of the screw bit deep into the ground. She looped the rope through and stood, tugging on it, testing the strength of the hook's placement. It would have to do.

She unclipped her climbing harness and stepped out of it, adjusting it and tugging it onto Sofia, over her shorts. She then fed the rope down, under Sofia's t-shirt, tying off the end on the harness to keep her in place on the rope. She stood, grasped the rope, and lifted Sofia off the ground, satisfied at how her head lolled away from the rope as she hung above the ledge. She set her down again and peered over the edge.

"Almost ready, Nick. She's going to be heavy. She's out cold. I'm just going to get something to protect her head."

Jess darted back into the shadow and scrabbled around inside her bag. She dug out the other half of the t-shirt she'd torn to strap her leg and tied it around Sofia's head. After feeding the rope through the securing hook, she gradually lowered the end to Nick. He grasped it out of the air and held tightly.

Jess cupped her hands around her mouth and shouted, "Do you remember how to feed it through your harness, like I showed you?"

Nick doubled the rope over in his hand and stared at it. "I think so," he called out, and began to feed it through. When he had adjusted it, he pulled another yard through, giving himself some slack, then tested it against the locking device. "I think I have it."

Jess smiled, blinking away more tears. "Good. Good. Now…you need to take all the slack through the harness now, because the rope is going to pull through as Sofia comes down. So, take as much as you can, okay?"

Nick nodded and began to work the rope through.

The process lasted less than a minute, but seemed to drag on for hours, as Jess' eyes flitted one way and the other, waiting for it to come back.

"Okay, I'm done." Nick called out. Jess pulled at the rope, happy with the tension. She put her arms under Sofia's armpits and shifted her to the edge of the ledge. "Lock off the rope now, Nick. I'm going to move her over the ledge."

She watched as Nick pulled the rope taut to one side, holding it with both hands. He nodded to show that he was ready, his body positioned to take the dead weight. Jess eased Sofia forward and gasped as she lurched down. The rope swung outward, her chin colliding with it and bouncing away. Then she was steady, turning gently with the rotation of the cord.

Jess exhaled. "Bring her down, Nick. *Slowly!*"

Nick began to let out the rope, Sofia's lifeless form gradually creeping down the rock wall. He paused now and then, when her head came close to the jagged edge, then started again. After a few minutes, she was suspended out over the bulk of the overhang, the wall much further from her. Nick sped up, allowing the rope to creep through his hands in a steady motion, until she hung just a handful of feet above him.

A growl sounded from behind him. He glanced around, but was unable to see properly in his position. "Jess…"

"I heard it. It's just a little further."

The sound got louder, a stomach-churning rumble, causing Nick's ribs to vibrate in his chest. He turned back to Sofia and eased her further down, towards him.

He felt the presence of the thing, behind him in the cavern. Rocks shifted beneath it as it moved closer. He turned his head again, still nothing showing up in the beam of his torch.

"Keep going!" Jess called from the ledge.

Nick lowered Sofia another couple of feet, then locked off the rope. He stepped forward and reached out for her, allowing the rope to slip through his harness. She lolled into his arms, and he held her close, scrunching his eyes closed in relief. He lowered her to the ground in the halo of lamplight and stood back up.

Having unclipped his harness, he let it fall to the ground before turning around and finding the source of the sound. His one-time hero stood in front of him, hunched over, skin and hair grey and thin. It parted its narrow lips and snarled. Nick watched as the creature's fingers flexed, flesh so tight to the bone they were almost indistinguishable from one another, fingernails missing altogether.

"Nick!" Jess' voice from above. "You have to help me down. You can't face him alone. You can't—"

The thing pounced forward, hands raised. It dove, forearm finding Nick's collarbone, knocking him off balance and pinning him to the ground. Nick heaved, the wind knocked out of him. He felt the strong thumbs of the creature working their way inward and pressing at his neck. He struggled, jerking his body left and right, trying to heave the thing off, but he didn't have the strength.

The creature's eyes narrowed, mouth open, as if ready to bite at Nick's sweat-slicked neck.

"Nicholas," Nick managed to spit the word out.

The thing froze, eyes widened. The light in its eyes changed. From the look of a determined predator to one of confusion or perhaps understanding.

"Nicholas Jones," Nick spoke more firmly now.

The thing shifted back on its haunches, releasing its grip on his shoulders. It released a drone-like groaning sound. Nick reached into the pocket of his cargo trousers and removed the bent cross and the photo Jess had recovered. He held them in front of him, watched as the creature's stare bore into them. It opened its mouth, the stub of its long-missing tongue jolted forward, carrying with it that hot, foul breath.

Nick brought his free hand to his chest. "I am…your grandson. Nicholas. Jones."

The thing reared up, letting out a scream that seemed to slice into Nick's skull. Then it disappeared into the darkness.

CHAPTER TWENTY-EIGHT

Nick's hands were quaking as he untangled the rope from his harness, Jess' feet safely on the ground. "Your knee," he said, gesturing with one trembling hand.

"It's not serious. The blood makes it look much worse. The bruise tomorrow will be impress—"

Before she could finish, the ground began to shake, almost knocking them both off balance.

"Another tremor?!" Jess squatted down beside Sofia, ready to shield her from falling debris, if required.

"Maybe. Or Al's guys digging us out." Nick pulled out the sat phone and checked the display.

No missed calls. He tapped in James' mobile number. Dialled. No response. The ground stilled, but the distant rumbling sound continued.

"We have to get to the entrance," Jess hooked Sofia's limp arm around her shoulder and lifted her up. "Come on."

"Do you need me to help carry her?"

"Just bring my pack. And the lantern. Go up in front, in case that thing comes back."

They left the cavern, Nick in front, with a pack over each shoulder. He held the lantern out in front, as if it could ward off that dark creature, as well as the gloom itself.

"Not too fast!" Jess called out. "These uphill tunnels are going to be a nightmare with sleeping beauty here on my shoulder. And that *thing* could be behind us, for all we know."

Nick slowed his pace and sharpened his focus on the space all around them as they ascended. The sound of the digging machines only grew as they progressed through the mineshafts. When they stopped for Jess to take a rest at the second level drop room, the noise was all-consuming. Jess mouthed words at Nick but was met with a quizzical expression. She stormed across the narrow chamber and dug out her water flask, taking a long drink. She fastened the lid and tossed it back across to Nick. He mouthed the word 'sorry' and stowed it back inside, before taking a swig from his own.

He stashed the bottle and moved to Jess' side. "She still hasn't come round."

"She'll be okay." Jess ran her fingers through Sofia's short, feathery hair.

"Want me to carry her the last couple of floors?"

Jess closed her eyes and shook her head. "I should never have let her run away. I'm going to make sure she gets out of this in one piece."

Nick had no response to that. He hurried back to the packs and heaved them onto his back. The lantern hanging from his outstretched hand, he nodded as if to check Jess was prepared, and they began the steep path up towards the entrance.

CHAPTER TWENTY-NINE

As he neared the top of the sloping pathway, the throaty noise of the digging machines continued its assault on Nick's ears. He squinted, holding the lantern to one side. Even with nightfall long past, he realised he could discern between the dark inside and that of the world beyond the mine, peeking through the newly-made cracks of the collapsed wall. He checked his watch. More than thirteen hours down here in the dark. Imagine what sixty years might do to your eyes. Much less your sanity.

"We should stay back," Nick said, pausing and opening his arms. "In case the ceiling collapses near the entrance."

"Good point. Can you put one of the packs down on the ground, so I've something soft to lower Sofia's head onto?"

Nick placed one of the bags down and kicked rocks away, creating space for Jess to lower Sofia to the ground.

She groaned as her body touched the cold floor, her eyes fluttering open. "What the fuck? Jess?" she said, her voice strained. She jerked her neck, trying to sit up.

Jess pressed her back down onto the bag. "He's gone for now. It's okay."

"He strung me up there. I was struggling, trying to stay conscious…but—"

"He caught you in the temple. We saw the video. You could've been killed," said Nick, perched over her prone body.

"Video? My god, my camera! All the footage!"

"We've got it. It seems fine. But we have to stick together now, until they can dig us out of here." He gestured towards the entrance, where the sound of the machines had quieted and shouting voices now crept in with the clinking of hand tools. "It shouldn't be long."

"Nick, I think I just heard someone call for you." Jess was standing at her full height, straining towards the collapsed entrance.

"Nick!" Al's voice, muffled but definitely present, came from the other side of the wall.

Nick squeezed Sofia's hand and hurried towards the barrier of rubble. "Al, what is it?" he called up towards the single hole in the mass of rock.

"Nick, we've had to shut down the machines. All these collapses have left the entrance seriously unstable. We're going to have to dig you a way out by hand. But it's going to be quite high up, on your side."

"Okay. Is there anything we can do from this side?"

"Without tools, not really. But listen, what kinda shape is Sofia in? You're going to need to move pretty fast. I can't promise how long it'll be before it all comes down."

"She's actually just come round. I think—" Nick looked back and saw the pale skin and burnished eyes of his grandfather creeping towards Jess. He called her name and burst into a run, desperate to close the gap between himself and his two companions.

Jess looked up and, as if she understood, twisted her body as she stood.

Nick could only watch as the thing flung itself towards her, catlike. Jess lowered her body, leading with her shoulder and transferring the explosive energy of its movement into a throw. The creature tried to wheel around, arms extended, bony, calloused fingers groping at her arms and shoulder for something to grab onto. Jess shifted backward, and the thing slammed hard into the rock wall, letting out a wail that had nothing in common with a human voice.

It righted itself on the ground, squatting on its haunches and growled. Nick altered his direction, heading instead directly for his grandfather. Jess stood ready, clutching a chunk of rock. Moments before Nick made impact, the thing leapt backward, fingers and toes engaging on the rock wall, and it scrambled over to the ceiling. Like a spider, it crossed the indented surface with speed and agility. Nick joined Jess, and they trained their eyes on it.

Jess took aim and launched the stone.

The thing swerved to avoid the rock, which clattered noisily against the roof and thumped back down a few yards from them.

Jess crouched, scooping up a handful of sharp-edged stones. "Have you got any more of those flares?" she said to Nick as she stood and wound up to throw another rock.

Nick shook his head. "They've both been used."

Jess let fly with another rock, then another. A volley of missiles soared towards the creature. One struck it on the midriff. The thing hissed, but continued its traverse of the cave roof, unabated. As it reached the other side, it placed a hand on the far wall and allowed itself to fall, making a neat landing on the other side of Sofia.

Sofia, her senses returning to her, scrabbled backwards, still prone on the ground.

"It's going to try to take her back!" screamed Jess. She was already sprinting towards Nick's grandfather.

It crouched into a compact shape, as though ready to pounce.

Jess twisted her head torch as she crossed the cavern, intensifying the light to its brightest setting. The thing shielded its eyes, maintaining its folded shape. Jess leapt towards it, the rounded toe of her boot seemingly dragging her across the space towards the thing's head. The creature unfolded itself, its reactions quick as a lizard's, bringing up one of the crudely fashioned meat hooks and slashing at Jess' calf.

The wail she produced as the tarnished metal ripped into her flesh turned Nick's stomach. Then it was buried by a rumbling that filled the cave. The earth was shaking. A gap appeared at the upper leftmost part of the collapsed entrance, and the bright beam of a floodlight shone in. A voice boomed through the gap, muffled by the distance and buried by the sustained sound of the quaking earth.

Nick glanced up at the entryway and then back at Jess. Blood oozed from the ragged flesh. The blue-white fingers of the creature wrapped around Sofia's ankles and pulled. She slid along the rock towards it. Jess was weeping now, desperately trying to hold Sofia back. Sofia kicked and thrashed with her legs, but it was too strong.

Nick ran his fingers through his hair, his heart thumping in his chest. He felt so powerless. Then something caught his eye. He dashed past the monster towards the downward tunnels. He grabbed the lantern by its handle and turned the dial, the flame growing as it drank in more of the fuel. Satisfied, he sprinted towards his grandfather and swung his arm back. He brought the lantern down on the back of the thing's head. Shards of glass flew off in all directions, catching the rescuers' light from the entrance like a million tiny snowflakes.

The flames took hold. The thin straggle of hair reaching down from the creature's withered skull burned up, the smell of charred hair overpowering. The skin on his head, back, and shoulders, slick with oil, ignited too, their flames almost transparent.

Realising what was happening, the creature jerked its body, dove for the floor, and thrashed around.

"Come on," said Nick. "We have to get Sofia out!"

Jess nodded and tried to stand. The ruin of her calf gave way on her, and she clattered to the ground. She shook her head and blinked away more tears. "I don't think… I can't stand."

Nick glanced up to see the creature, still rolling on the ground, trying desperately to extinguish the flames that ravaged its back.

"Stay here. Keep an eye on him. I'll be as quick as I can," he said, looping Sofia's arm around his shoulder and gingerly lifting her to a standing position.

The ground continued to rumble, sending Nick and Sofia careening as he supported her slowly towards the exit.

"What about Jess?" Sofia's voice was ragged, uneven.

"I'm going back for her. The second we get you out." Nick glanced over his shoulder, relieved that his grandfather remained on the floor, trying desperately to douse the flames that engulfed him.

Sofia groaned, but quickened her pace.

They reached the base of the collapsed rock wall. The floodlight that had been pouring into the mine was now partly obscured by a heavyset man in a fluorescent jacket.

Sofia reached up, as if looking for stable rock to climb towards the hole. It was hard to tell which of the boulders that blocked the entrance were moving and which stuck in place, with the shaking of the earth beneath them. She scampered up, then slipped backward as rocks skittered beneath her feet.

Nick pressed into her back with outstretched hands. "Push back against me if you have to. It's not far."

She clambered up a little higher, then placed one of her feet on Nick's outstretched hand. Using him as a support, she bound up to the top, locking her forearm into the outstretched, grasping hand of the paramedic.

"I've got you," the medic said. "It's okay now."

Before he could move her onto the platform of the cherry picker where he stood, Sofia turned. Her eyes met Nick's. "Bring Jess back. Please. Go!"

Nick turned and dashed across the cavernous entrance, keeping his centre of gravity low to the ground so as to keep his balance against the trembling earth. He arrived at Jess' side and reached out for her, placing his arm around her waist. She placed her arm around his shoulder and put her weight on him.

"Are you sure you can't stand?" Nick's eyes were drawn to Jess' torn calf as he asked the question.

"Let's find out," she said and gave him a quiet count of three.

They each pushed upward, Jess' full weight bearing down on Nick's shoulders. She screamed and grimaced as the muscle tried to support the weight, almost falling onto Nick.

Sweat barrelled down Nick's face. "I don't think I can carry you."

"Fucking drag me, Nick. It doesn't matter, just get us out of here before the whole thing comes down. Or worse."

He strode forward, his arms hooked around Jess' waist. She allowed her right leg to scrape along the ground, the injured left flailing on top of it. Nick did his best to block out the sound of Jess weeping, risking only fleeting glances over his shoulder as the blue-white skin of the creature charred and bubbled as it writhed on the ground.

They arrived at the bottom of the sloping pile of rubble that led to the exit. Fine dust and particles of rock fell in a sporadic stream from several points in the ceiling now. The walls at either side of the entrance were cracking, boulders of increasingly large sizes breaking off, some getting caught in the protective mesh that lined the walls, others coming loose and smashing into the rock floor, either whole or crumbling to pieces.

"I'm not going to make it up there, Nick. It's too steep. My leg." Jess reached down and clutched at the wound.

Nick lowered her to the ground and untied the makeshift bandage covering her knee. He pulled it across the ragged calf and pulled it taut. Jess screamed. "It has to be tight. I'm going to lift you up there."

"Nick you ca—"

"It's only a few yards to the exit. It'll be okay. Lean into my shoulder."

Jess did as she was asked, and Nick boosted her up, angling his body forward to balance the weight. He pulled her legs in tight to his torso, careful to avoid the injury and took gradual steps up the pile of rubble.

"Nick, hurry," she said, her voice muffled by his shoulder.

"I *am* hurrying. This is almost impossible." He grunted as he tried to shift up a gear.

"No, I mean *hurry*. He's put the fire out. He's coming!"

Nick managed a look over his shoulder and immediately regretted it. The hair on the creature's head was gone, skin and much of the muscle burned away like the wax on a candle. Like a charred skeleton, it staggered forward now, eyes narrowed and focussed on the two of them.

Nick took a breath and strode upward. He heaved Jess further up towards the exit, then had to lower her to the surface of the rubble as he ran out of strength. "I'm sorry," he said. "I don't know if I can…"

The whirring sound of the cherry picker's platform sounded outside the hole in the entrance wall. The paramedic squeezed the upper part of his torso through and reached towards Jess. "Can you get to me? Or take my hand?"

Jess motioned towards her leg, now wrapped in the torn, bloodstained fabric of her vest. "I don't know. I'll try." She reached out.

Nick took another step forward and placed his arms around her torso, lifting her up just a little further. The strong hands of the paramedic clasped around hers and pulled her forward, Jess groaning and placing as much weight as possible on her good leg. Once close enough, the paramedic scooped her over his shoulder and out through the narrow gap.

"I'll be back for you as soon as I can," he told Nick as he began to descend.

Nick glanced back to find his grandfather still creeping and stumbling towards him despite his ragged state. The ground beneath Nick's feet trembled and a large rock dropped from the ceiling, almost smashing the bags. Everything they'd collected. The documents, the video camera with all that high-definition footage. He felt in his trouser pocket where he still had the bent cross and the two photos from his grandfather's alcove.

It wasn't enough.

Nick sprang forward, his legs and arms heavy with lactic acid from the considerable effort of moving each of the girls up the sloping pile of boulders. At the bottom of the makeshift ramp of stones, he broke into a run and reached the bags in a matter of moments. He swept one up onto each shoulder, then threw himself to one side, narrowly avoiding another falling rock.

"Hey!" The paramedic was back at the entrance, waving his arms. "The place is going to come down. The engineer out here says five minutes, tops! Come on!"

Nick climbed to his feet and hurried back towards the pile of rock and the exit. He reached out with his hands and began to scramble upward, eyes locked on the paramedic and his outstretched hands, promising safety. The earth shook with renewed vigour almost knocking Nick off balance, but he managed to stay upright, scaling another few feet by reaching for a craggy piece of stone with his outstretched left hand. As he did, a crack overhead caused him to look up. He froze as a fragment of the ceiling, perhaps a foot across, tumbled and crash-landed on his trailing right leg.

Nick screamed in pain, but refused to allow it to shift his focus. He shoved at the rock with both hands. It refused to budge. He tried to squeeze the leg out from underneath. The weight was too great, the angle impossible. Then he saw how close his grandfather was. The monster lumbered towards him, charred, sinewy flesh flexing with every step. Nick shook his head, biting down on his bottom lip as he tried to hold it together.

The creature jutted forward, fixing its claw-like hands around the edges of the boulder. It bored into Nick's eyes with its own. Nick swallowed, ready for the inevitable. The thing clenched its muscles and hauled the rock off Nick's leg. Nick squirmed backwards, pain shooting up his leg, which hung limply from the knee joint down. The thing gestured to the hole in the entrance wall and emitted a low, pained wail.

Nick dragged himself and the bags up the sloping pile of boulders. The paramedic reached in, secured Nick around his upper torso, and heaved him out.

As the cherry picker's basket descended to ground level, the mine entrance collapsed completely, the arching entry no longer recognisable. Al was waiting at ground level, an ambulance parked beside his van, with Jess and Sofia both under foil blankets on gurneys. They waved towards Nick, and he smiled despite the agony.

Still being supported by the strong paramedic, he held up the bags with the cameras and documents inside. It was over. They had what they had come for. And they'd made it out...alive.

CHAPTER THIRTY

Six Months Later...

Nick pulled at his bow tie, sure it was constricting him. The ugly buildings around the airport hotel where he'd spent the night had given way to the glitzy lights of the strip. He gazed out of the taxi's window as he pulled up in front of the movie theatre.

The driver moved around, opening the door, and guiding Nick towards James, whose arms were wide open for an embrace. The two men hugged, James slapping Nick on the back and chuckling.

"Here we are then," said Nick, allowing himself a smile.

"Here we are," said James, sunglasses reflecting the early evening sun into Nick's eyes.

"There were times, you know, when I didn't think..."

"I know. But we did it. *You* did it."

"Are the others...?"

The question hung in the air momentarily before an elegantly-dressed Sofia came dashing towards him, arms open for another hug. Jess was close behind, jogging despite the dress and heels that had her towering over him.

"So happy to see you!" Sofia said as she squeezed him.

"I can't even tell you." Nick's words were almost inaudible as he exhaled.

"Foot seems all right?" said Jess, reaching in for her own hug.

"Two steel pins through the ankle. And an *enormous* scar. But it's better now, yep. How are you guys?"

"We're doing great. Much better since this one relocated here." Sofia clasped Jess' hand in her own and kissed it.

"Did you get a show?"

Jess beamed, her cheeks reddening.

"She's got a five-year contract," James said, stepping into the huddle. "We *loved* what she did with you guys. So we're sending her off to a new find in Ecuador. Ancient civilisations, ruined temples—"

"—short shorts," interrupted Sofia.

Jess pulled a face. "All the better for my camera operator, right?"

The two of them giggled.

"That's amazing. And well deserved. What about the museum? And the show?" Nick smiled at James but wondered how transparent his nerves were.

"The museum is almost finished. The subterranean parts we scoped out before we met had to be scrapped. I don't think I need to go into why. But it's a great legacy project—and great publicity for the channel, I'm not afraid to admit."

Nick's smile grew warmer, easier. "And the show? The narrative? The whole reason I did this..."

"Your grandpa is the hero of this story. From what you guys found, we pieced it together. Reconstructions, spliced with your footage—and our voiceover guy—you're going to love him." James placed his arm around Nick's shoulder and led him towards the theatre, Jess and Sofia keeping pace with them.

As they stepped from the blazing sun into the shade of the theatre foyer, Nick stopped. "But what about the journal? The footage? What he did to Sofia?"

Sofia released Jess' hand and took Nick's instead. "That wasn't him. That was something else. Maybe a crude sort of man, debased to living on instinct. Maybe something other. Doesn't change what he did in '57. Doesn't change the fact that he used his last breath to help you out of that hellhole."

A runner appeared, swing doors swooshing shut behind her. "Press are seated. Screening starts in five." She hurried from sight as fast as she'd arrived.

Their eyes met, a smile tugging at James' lips. "We chose which elements of your grandfather's story to tell. Desperation is something our viewers will appreciate." Then he whispered, "creatures that defy everything an eighty-year-old man ought to be capable of, not so much. Don't worry."

Nick nodded his head, thoughtfully. He leaned against the door to the auditorium. "Let's not keep our public waiting, shall we?"

ACKNOWLEDGMENTS

Below would not have been half the story it is today, were it not for the diligent, insightful beta reading of Dave Watkins (*The Original's Return*) and Dan Howarth (*Dark Missives*). I hope to be able to repay that debt in beer once post-pandemic normality is achieved.

I'd also like to thank Ken McKinley at Silver Shamrock for believing in the story and Kenneth Cain for sharpening up the manuscript immeasurably.

Thanks, as ever, must also go out to fellow writers who have supported me from the get go, such as Stephanie Ellis, Alyson Faye, Grant Longstaff, TC Parker, Ross Jeffery, CC Adams, Thomas Joyce, Erik Hofstatter, Steve Dillon, Dave Jeffery, Hailey Piper, Shane Douglas Keene, Tabatha Wood, Steve Stred, Catherine McCarthy, Laurel Hightower, Simon Paul Wilson, Brian Bowyer, Beverley Lee, Paul Feeney, Luke Kondor, Bob Pastorella, Joshua Marsella, Christopher Stanley, Calvin Demmer, Dean Drinkel, S. J. Budd, Joanna Koch, Jeremy Hepler, Joshua Marsella, J. A. Sullivan and Ruschelle Dillon.

Special thanks, too, to the review sites, book bloggers, bookstagrammers, and BookTubers who have given their time to review and promote my work, such as Kendall Reviews, The Ginger Nuts of Horror, Sublime Horror, Hellhound Magazine, Yvonne of The Coy Caterpillar Reads, Sadie Hartmann (aka Mother Horror), Rebbie Reviews, Well Read Beard, J of J Maddux Entertainment, Nichi of Dark Between Pages, and Raul of Raul Reads.

Final thanks go out to the readers who part with their money and time to read my work. It means more than you can possibly know.

ABOUT THE AUTHOR

Kev Harrison is a British writer of horror and dark fiction, living on the outskirts of Lisbon, Portugal. His debut collection, *Paths Best Left Untrodden* is available now from Northern Republic. His novella, *The Balance*, a reimagining of the Slavic folk tale of Baba Yaga set in cold war Poland, is also available. When he's not writing dark tales, Kev can be found running, sampling too many craft beers for his own good, singing bizarre songs to his cats, and travelling to far flung places with his better half, Ana. You can find him at www.kevharrisonfiction.com or on Twitter as @LisboetaIngles

ALSO AVAILABLE FROM
SILVER SHAMROCK PUBLISHING

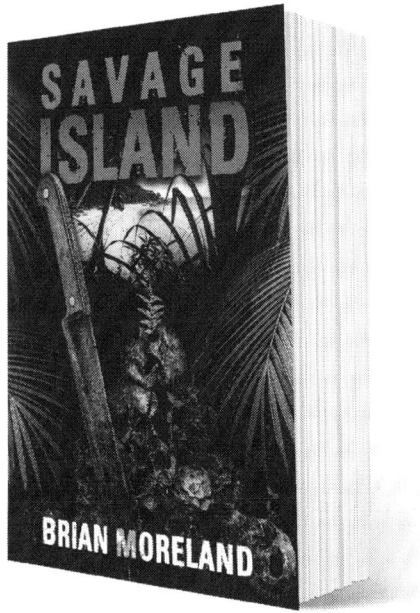

Terror in tropical paradise

On an isolated island in the Philippines, it patiently waits. A mysterious terror lurks in the shadows, stalking the poor stranded souls who visit the island. When a group of four tourists find their vacation quickly turning into a nightmare, the terror taunts them and comes for them one by one. The sandy beach and crystal waters of the lagoon will run red with blood if they can't find a way off this savage island.

ALSO AVAILABLE FROM
☘ SILVER SHAMROCK PUBLISHING ☘

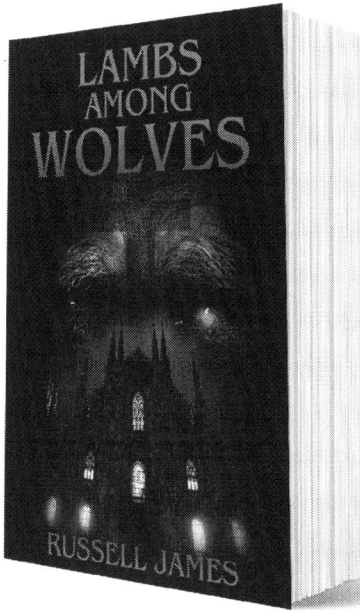

Evil may soon consume mankind, if the demons have their way.

After the death of her father, young Cyndi Fisher travels to Paris to meet the grandfather she never knew. That man turns out to be Father Jack Cahill, a renegade exorcist who was unaware he'd fathered a child before taking his vows.

Cyndi is soon drawn into Father Jack's world, where demons from Hell are possessing humans and robbing Europe's churches of sacred relics. From the cathedrals of Paris, through the graveyards of France, and into the sewers of Rome, they confront the possessed, battle risen corpses, and fight gang members sent to stop them.

They uncover a plot to set Satan free upon the Earth, but stopping it seems impossible. Demons are always one step ahead of them, and each manifestation is more powerful than the last. Stopping Satan's return will take courage and faith. Will an aged priest and an agnostic teen have enough of either?

ALSO AVAILABLE FROM
SILVER SHAMROCK PUBLISHING

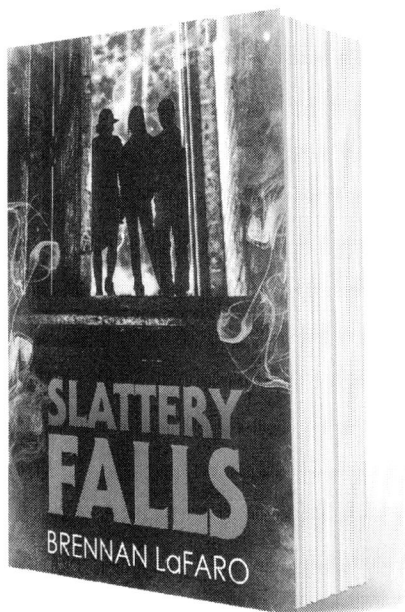

Travis, Elsie, and Josh, college kids with a ghost-hunting habit, scour New England for the most interesting haunted locales. Their journey eventually leads them to Slattery Falls, a small Massachusetts town living in the shadow of the Weeks House. The former home of the town's most sinister and feared resident sits empty. At least that's what the citizens say. It's all in good fun. But after navigating the strange home, they find the residents couldn't be more wrong. And now the roles are reversed. The hunters have become the hunted. Something evil refuses to release its grip, forcing the trio into one last adventure.

Printed in Great Britain
by Amazon

65585424R00092